Crime afte

Crime after Crime

a collection of crime stories

Edited by Debz Hobbs-Wyatt and Stephen Puleston

Bridge House

British Library Cataloguing in Publication Data

A Record of this Publication is available from the British Library

ISBN 978-1-907335-24-2

This edition published 2012 by Bridge House Publishing
Manchester, England

Contents

Foreword

Stephen Leather

What makes a good short story? To answer that question, I did what most writers do these days when they do their research – I Googled it.

And the answer? Well, the consensus is that you need a clearly defined plot line made up of an exposition (supplying background information); rising action (events in the story that lead to a climax); a climax (some event or events that pull the rising actions together); falling actions (events that result from the climax); and a cohesive resolution, where the entire story is pulled together to form a logical conclusion.

That, I'm afraid, is called writing by numbers, and is as much a recipe for a disaster as it is for producing a great short story.

I'm best known for my full-length thrillers but I've tried my hand at writing short stories and hand on heart I can tell you that short stories are harder to write than novels. Seriously. It's far easier to tell a story over 120,000 words than 10,000.

With a novel, it's all about what you put in. With a short story, what you leave out is just as important. Maybe more so. With a novel you have time to develop sub-plots that tide you over when the main story starts to flag. If you don't describe a character perfectly the first time, you get the chance to revisit them later in the book. But a short story is a diamond that is polished until it's perfect. Every word has to count. The story has to be faultless, the characters perfectly-drawn and the pace unflagging. You have so few words to play with that any flaws are easy to spot.

Crime After Crime contains twelve short stories that were selected from more then two hundred submissions. I have nothing but admiration for those writers who made the final cut. They all have one thing at common. They are all written from the heart, which is what good-storytelling is about. It's not about following formulas or recipes, it's about producing stories with fascinating characters in situations that set the pulse racing. They are stories that get you inside the heads of heroes and villains alike and allow you to experience life in the raw.

Bridge House Publishing offers new writers a way of getting their work out to the wider world and I'm sure that many of the writers in this collection will be much better known in the future. And from my experience I think they'll find writing full-length novels easier.

About the author

Stephen Leather was a journalist for more than ten years on newspapers such as *The Times*, *Daily Mail* and the *South China Morning Post* in Hong Kong. Before that, he was employed as a biochemist for ICI, shovelled limestone in a quarry, worked as a baker, a petrol pump attendant, a barman, and worked for the Inland Revenue. He began writing full time in 1992. His bestsellers, including the *Spider Shepherd* series and super-natural detective Jack Nightingale series, have been translated into more than ten languages. He has also written for television shows such as *London's Burning*, *The Knock* and the BBC's *Murder in Mind* series. You can find out more from his website, www.stephenleather.com.

Blood in Summer

Sam Millar

I held the coffee cup rigid at my mouth as I read the morning's headline: **Murder Case To Be Re-opened.**

"Tom?" Belinda, my wife, interrupted my thoughts. "You okay?"

"Heartburn."

"You sure?"

"Yes." I smiled falsely, returning to the photo in the newspaper, while thinking back to all those years ago…

Mid-June, the town in a heat wave. I was skinny-dipping in Jackson's Lake with my two best friends, Paul Fleming and Charlie Redden. The lake could be deceptively still at times, but quite crafty in its nature. Police danger signs were posted everywhere.

I'd just stepped out of the water when I spotted a figure on top of the hill.

"That looks like Joey Maxwell," I said, pointing.

Paul glanced towards the hill.

"You're right, Tommy. It's him."

"How many times have we told him he can't hang with us?" asked Charlie.

Joey was twelve – two years younger than us – so there was no way we could be seen with a kid. Besides, the horrible episode from last year was still fresh in our minds, and even though it wasn't Joey's fault, we no longer felt comfortable when he was anywhere near us.

"Joey! What the hell're you doing!" shouted Paul.

Joey didn't reply, inching slowly into the water.

"He's going for a dip, with his clothes on," said Charlie, grinning. "Go on, Joey! You can do it!"

Suddenly, we were all chanting, "Joey! Joey! Joey!"

9

Every deliciously fear-charged moment of entertainment increased, as water moved up to Joey's neck.

We began counting out the seconds, daring him to break the all-time record of one minute and ten seconds for staying under the water.

"One, two, three…"

He was gone.

We continued counting in a drum roll.

"Twenty, twenty-one…"

On and on we counted, our voices rising with each fading second.

"Fifty-nine, *sixtyyyyyyyyy*! Sixty-one, sixty two…"

At seventy, our voices slowly filtered out, leaving a heavy silence.

"Someone's gotta dive in there, see what that he's up to," said Paul. "Tommy?"

"Why me?"

"You're the best swimmer."

I didn't want to be part of anything that might have happened under that dirty water, but I had little choice.

For some inexplicable reason, the water felt colder as my bare feet touched it. Seconds later, I was in, propelling my body downwards in the murky thickness. Visibility became nil as I went deeper.

But it wasn't too long before panic began building up inside my burning lungs. I needed to resurface. Then, just as I twisted my body to head upwards, an old wreck of a car mistily came into view. Ghostly green, its smashed windows looked like gaping eyes. I wanted to swim away from it, but its magnetic pull drew me closer.

That was when I spotted Joey, motionless. He seemed to be gripping the car.

I went torpedoing forward, reached out and took hold of his arm. He didn't move, his face expressionless in the godless gloom of watery darkness.

Quickly grabbing the back of his shirt, I began yanking as hard as I could.

Nothing. His body resisted.

I pulled some more on the shirt, but my lungs were on fire. I quickly swam to the surface, empty-handed, gulping on the beautiful taste of air.

"Get help!" I shouted, before plunging back down.

Under the water, I tried searching for the wreck, but the water was becoming murkier. I found nothing, other than a forest of thick weeds. I tried swimming through them, but suddenly they began entwining themselves on my legs. It felt like someone trying to hold me down.

Panicking, I kicked out at the weeds, but their grip became iron. Water began rushing into my mouth.

No! Not like this! I screamed in my head. *Don't die like this...*

I remember Charlie dragging me back to land, but that was about all I recalled. "He's... he's down there, Charley," I spluttered, coughing up water.

"Paul's away to get help. It'll be okay." Charlie was lighting a cigarette. I could tell from the way his hands were shaking he understood it was anything but okay.

By the time an ambulance arrived in tandem with a police jeep, I knew it was too late. Joey was gone. I also knew I was in trouble, as I watched the sheriff emerging from the jeep, rushing towards me.

"Are you okay, Tommy?" The sheriff quickly bent down beside me.

"Joey's down there, Dad."

"Don't worry. We'll find him," said Dad, before running in the direction of police divers.

I knew Dad would have more to say to me, later. He didn't agree with my friendship of Paul, whom he

11

regarded as a future felon.

It took the divers forty minutes to locate Joey, but two hours to bring his body to the surface. He'd handcuffed himself to the steering wheel of the old wreck – the same handcuffs his father used as a prison guard for years.

The newspaper headlines suggested Joey's suicide had been triggered because of a sexual attack on him. They also noted, ominously, that his attacker had never been apprehended, even though police had a suspect but couldn't arrest him through lack of evidence.

The papers took a picture of me. They said I was a hero trying to save a drowning pal.

"That bastard, Not Normal. He killed Joey," said Paul.

"*Shhhh!*" I hissed, looking nervously behind my shoulder. "Only a few people know Not Normal's a suspect. If my dad finds out I was listening to his phone conversations, I'll be in for it."

Not Normal – Norman Armstrong – acquired the moniker after his name being repeatedly pronounced wrongly by every kid in town, usually when entering the movie house where the creepy loner worked.

Normal, can you tell us if there's a cartoon on today? Will the ice-cream woman be working today, Normal? Normal, can you tell me—

This went on for months, until one night, he had had enough. *I'm Norman!* he screamed, in utter frustration, making history eternally with the following classic statement: *I'm not fucking Normal!*

"They should shoot the perv," continued Paul, so serious it scared me.

"Yea, in the head," said Charlie.

"We should make a pact, like they do in the movies," continued Paul, who loved nothing better than a good murder movie. "Are you game, Tommy?"

"For what?"

"Justice for Joey. We take an oath, right here." He held out his hand and with the other produced a penknife. "A blood oath."

"I..." Even though I believed nothing would come of this so-called blood oath, the hairs on the back of my neck suddenly nipped my skin. "Okay..."

Paul held out his thumb, curving the knife inwards. The skin tore. An inkblot of blood appeared. I would never forget it. Dirty crimson. Like the bloodshot eye of a trapped animal.

"Here," said Paul, handing the knife to me, while holding his bloody thumb outwards.

I took the knife, cut.

"Now you, Charlie," commanded Paul.

Charlie cut.

"Put all our thumbs together," said Paul.

We complied.

"Let the oath of blood brothers and secrecy live with us..." continued Paul, forcing the three thumbs tightly against each other, allowing the blood to mingle. "Forever."

For the longest time of my life, I waited to take my thumb away. It felt on fire.

"Are we finished?" I finally asked. "I've got to head home. I'm still under curfew."

"Finished," said Paul. "Give me time to think out a plan."

There would be no plan, of course, just Paul living out one of his fantasies.

The next day, I met Paul and Charlie at the bottom of my street.

"I've something I want to show you," said Paul.

"What?"

"You'll see. Let's head over to Blackwood."

13

Blackwood was the large forest area surrounding Jackson's Lake.

"This'll do," said Paul, thirty minutes later, stopping beside an old uprooted tree badly gone to rot.

I watched him dropping to his knees, digging at the soil. A few minutes later, he stood, a rag-covered package in his hand.

"What's that?" said Charlie.

Paul peeled the rag away, revealing a gun wrapped protectively in polythene. It stared out at us like a mummified foetus.

"*Whoa*! Is it *real*?" said Charlie.

"As real as your cock," said Paul, releasing the gun from the enclosure. "It's a German Luger."

I was less impressed, having seen plenty of guns in my life. By the time I was seven, I had handled my first gun. Yet, there was something different about this gun displayed proudly in Paul's hands. It sent the dual shivers of fear and weariness up my spine.

"Where'd you get it?" I asked.

"My granddad brought it back from the war."

This was a new Paul – a Paul with secrets. As friends, we weren't supposed to have secrets – at least not of this magnitude.

"Have you fired it?" asked Charlie.

"Old Mullan's barn. Almost shot one of his bulls."

"That's bullshit," said Charlie, grinning.

Without warning, Paul cocked the Luger. The sound made me think of someone's knuckles cracking. Slowly, he brought the gun up to Charlie's face.

"Think I'm a bullshitter, Charlie?"

Both Charlie and I went rigid. Fear spread through me, and everything began to tingle in a very bad way. I could see Paul's finger tightening on the trigger.

14

"Paul..." I finally managed to croak, my mouth dry as cotton. "Don't mess with—"

He pulled the trigger.

Kraaaaaaaaaaaaaaaacckk!

"You should've seen the look on your face, Charlie!" Paul was grinning like a frog. "It wasn't even loaded."

Charlie began retching violently.

Instinctively, I grabbed the gun from Paul's grip, and pushed him. He landed firmly on his butt.

"Are you fucking mad!" I shouted.

"It... it wasn't loaded," he mumbled.

Removing the magazine from the Luger's heel, I could see a bullet nestled on top. I slowly removed the bullet, and held it out.

"Wasn't fucking loaded! What's *that*?"

It was Paul's turn to look frightened.

"I thought it was empty..." he mumbled.

"Never point a gun at anyone, unless you intend to use it." I sounded like Dad in one of his daily lectures. I threw the gun and single bullet at Paul's feet, before turning to Charlie. "You okay?"

"Yes..." He nodded.

Paul stood, wiping dirt from his jeans. "You're right, Tommy, I shouldn't point a gun unless I'm willing to use it. Well, I'll be pointing it at Armstrong's head, once I get a plan set up."

It took Paul three days to come up with a plan. It was late when we sat on a small collection of rocks deep inside Blackwood.

"Every Thursday night after the movie house shuts, Armstrong takes porn movies home to watch in that run-down trailer of his," said Paul.

"How do you know?" asked Charlie.

15

"Everyone *knows*," said Paul, his voice rising slightly.

From the look on Charlie's face, he obviously wasn't everyone. I guess I wasn't everyone either, because I had the same look.

You're gonna be the bait, Charlie," said Paul.

"*Bait?*" Charlie frowned.

"Something to lure the perv to where we can get him off-guard."

"Why me?"

"Would you rather pull the trigger?"

"No..."

Almost immediately I realised I had underestimated Paul's conviction to this plan.

"We'll meet back here tomorrow night," continued Paul. "And remember: this is for Joey."

Armstrong's trailer was a rust bucket, parked just outside town. In the iron darkness, a faint light filtered from the trailer's back window.

For the last hour, we did a stakeout, just across from the trailer. As Paul predicted, Armstrong was home.

"You ready, Charlie?" asked Paul.

"Yes..."

"Know what to do?"

Charlie nodded. "Tap on his door, ask for directions. Tell him I'm lost and thirsty."

"It's important you say you're thirsty. Understand?"

"Yes."

I kept wondering when Paul was going to chicken out, believing his game-plan had to be relying on Charlie or me backing out first. That way, he would save face and still be king of the castle.

"We're gonna have to crawl from here, so he doesn't spot us," whispered Paul, dropping on his belly. "Come on."

Getting down, we crawled behind him like characters from an old war movie. A minute later, we reached the back of the trailer, and stood. Dull sounds were coming from inside.

Paul edged his face against the back window. "The perv's watching a porno. Check it out, Tommy."

Easing my face partially against the window, I focused with one eye. It was dark inside, but the luminous light from the television helped. Armstrong was sitting on a battered armchair, bottle of beer in one hand, remote control in the other. He seemed engrossed on whatever was on the television.

"Okay, Charlie. Make a move for the door," said Paul.

"You... you won't let him kill me, will you, Paul?"

"Don't be stupid. He's the one who's gonna be killed. Now move!"

Slowly, Charlie edged his body along the front of the trailer. Even in the dull moonlight, I could see the terror on his face.

What seemed like an eternity passed before Charlie began rapping timidly on the door.

I quickly glanced in at Armstrong. He hit a button on the remote, muting the television.

Charlie rapped again.

The door opened, bleaching Charlie in light.

"Yes?" said Armstrong.

"I'm... I'm lost, Mister," said Charlie. "Could... could you give me some directions on how to get home... please?"

"Where the hell's home, boy?"

"Fair... Fairbanks. I live in Fairbanks," lied Charlie.

"Fairbanks? You're a long way out. What're you do-ing in this neck of the woods?"

I could detect suspicion in Armstrong's voice.

"I... I was with a couple of friends, camping in

Blackwood, but we split up after a stupid argument," replied Charlie.

"Camping's illegal in Blackwood."

"You… you're not going to call the cops, are you?"

"No, so relax. Come in. You look hungry. You hungry, boy?"

"And thirsty…"

Everything went dark as the trailer door slammed.

"What now?" I asked.

"We wait until Armstrong comes to the back of the trailer. That's where he keeps his cola."

Paul eased his face along the window, eyeing the scene from a corner. I took the other corner.

I could see Charlie standing at the doorway. Armstrong was talking. Charlie looked petrified.

Suddenly, Armstrong turned, and looked directly at us. Paul and I ducked down immediately. Above, I could hear movement approaching, then the sound of a cupboard opening.

Paul eased his head back up, and peeped into the window. I followed suit and saw Armstrong taking a bottle of cola from an overhead cupboard. He eased the cap from the bottle.

A few seconds later, Armstrong poured the cola into a glass, then, using the opened cupboard door as a shield, he began adding a touch of clear liquid from a small container into the glass.

"What the hell's he doing?" I looked at Paul. He was gripping the Luger so tightly, his knuckles looked like they were ready to pop. I watched in horror as he brought the muzzle of the gun to the window, hands trembling terribly.

He's really going to shoot, I thought, watching him take shaky aim.

Without warning, Armstrong eased his face towards the window. I was certain he had spotted us. I froze.

Armstrong continued staring. It wasn't until later I realised he wasn't looking at us, but Charlie's mirrored image on the window.

Turning, Armstrong headed back down the trailer to Charlie.

"Paul? We can't let him do this to Charlie," I pleaded.

But Paul didn't respond. He simply stood there, like an android, pointing the gun at the window. It was then I noticed the enormous dark patch in Paul's washed-out jeans. He had pissed himself.

"Paul!" I screamed, not caring if Armstrong could hear us. "Snap out of it!"

"I... I... I..." His lips were barely moving.

"Shit!" I screamed, running towards the front of the trailer before kicking in the door.

Charlie looked relieved; Armstrong looked shocked.

"Run, Charlie!"

Outside, we ran quickly to the end of the trailer to get Paul, but he was already running in the opposite direction, towards Blackwood forest.

It was the last time I would ever see him...

Next day, I waited nervously as Dad returned home from night duty. I sat, pretending to read my comics.

"Not out enjoying the sun?" he asked.

"I want to finish this." I held up the copy of *Batman*.

So far so good. No mention of Armstrong.

"Are you still running about with that Fleming kid?"

My stomach suddenly did a little kick. Had he heard something, after all? Dad was very good at trapping people – just ask any of the criminals he had interrogated over the years before jailing them.

"I... won't be with him, anymore, Dad. That's a promise."

He gave me one of his ten-second stares before replying.

"Make sure you keep that promise. Now, get out into the fresh air."

I nodded, and headed for the door, grateful that the whole sorry Armstrong-episode was over with.

By the time I reached the lake, the sun was baking down on me. The place was deserted, and the cool calm water looked totally inviting. Despite warnings from Dad to stay out of the water, I couldn't resist. It still had that magnetic pull on me. Moreover, to overcome Joey's death, I knew I had to conquer the water first. It was the only way to stop the nightmares I was having of Joey's face, his skin being peeled and devoured by tiny fish.

Stripping, I began piling my clothes against some rocks, when suddenly I thought I spotted someone staring at me from the trees' shadows, deep beyond the lake's fringe.

"Paul? Is that you?"

Nothing.

"Who's there?"

I thought of Joey's ghost.

To hell with it. I ran naked towards the water's coolness, diving into its murky underworld. It was exhilarating, and I went deeper, testing lungs, resolve and nerve.

I seemed to have been swimming for hours when my head finally broke through the water's ceiling. Breathing deeply, I let a yell of joy scream from my mouth. "I'm alive!"

But the euphoria quickly dissipated when I heard something enter the water directly behind me.

To my dismay, it was a girl, her dark hair crapped-in like a pageboy. Her face was a constellation of freckles. Like me, she was totally naked. Unlike me, she was beautiful.

I felt my face burn. Had she seen me naked?

"What's your name?" she asked, nonchalantly, as if

seeing a naked boy was the norm.

I couldn't speak. The sight of her nipples, poking above the water line, hypnotised me. It was the first time I had ever seen a naked girl. It was thrilling and terrifying.

"Are you deaf?" she said. "What's your name?"

"Tommy," I finally managed to mumble, trying desperately to look away from her breasts, but failing miserably.

A smile appeared on her face. "I've seen you a couple of times, swimming here with your friends."

"You watched us, swimming…?" Nude, I wanted to say, but didn't.

"Out of sheer boredom, so don't get the wrong idea." The smile widened, making her even more beautiful. "Are you the one who discovered the dead kid?"

I nodded. "Joey… his name was Joey Maxwell."

"You must be very brave."

"I don't know," I said, shrugging my shoulders.

"I wish someone would do that for me."

"I would," I said, the two words sounding as if I had known her all my life.

She laughed loudly, but I detected sadness in the sound.

Suddenly, she disappeared underwater only to reappear seconds later beside me. Before I knew what was happening, she was kissing me full on the mouth. I could taste her breath, the saltiness of her tongue, the pressure of her breasts against my chest.

I gasped as I felt her hands began fondling my balls under the water, as if weighing them. I couldn't breathe. Her fingers moved across the shaft of my cock. I jerked back, as if being prodded by electricity.

"What's wrong? Haven't you been with a girl before?"

"Of course," I lied, feeling my face burn with embarrassment. "Lots."

She laughed. "I've got to go."

21

"Now? But…"

"Yes. Now."

"But…"

She began swimming towards where our clothes lay in a heap. I watched her easing out of the water, small buttocks seesawing mischievously.

"Aren't you coming, Tommy?"

I couldn't. Too terrified she would see my penis, all stiff and angry.

"I… no, I'm going to swim for a while."

"Okay."

I watched her putting on her clothing, preparing to leave.

"What's *your* name!" I shouted.

"Dakota."

"Will you be here, tomorrow?"

"Perhaps."

That night, I enjoyed the first good sleep since Joey's death. Instead of nightmares of him, I dreamt of a mysterious girl called Dakota, wondering when – *if* – I would see her again.

Next day I ran as fast as I could towards Jackson's Lake. Arriving at the exact spot from yesterday. I sat waiting. But my initial burst of euphoria quickly turned to despondency. She wasn't coming. Not now. Probably not ever. I'd been a fool to think someone so beautiful would have an interest in someone as plain and boring as me.

Four hours later, I eventually returned home, defeated.

For days I moped about the house until finally threatened by Dad.

"If you don't get out and go someplace, I'll be forced to bring you over to the jail to clean toilets."

Taking the hint, I left, walking in the direction of the lake, almost in a trance, hardly hearing Charlie behind me.

"Going for a swim, Tommy?"

"No. Just walking and killing time. What's happening?"

"Nothing much." Charlie looked embarrassed, as if he had been avoiding me. It seemed we were all involved in a conspiracy of avoidance.

"Seen Paul about?" I asked.

"Yesterday, for a few minutes. We didn't speak much. He..." Charlie peered over his shoulder. "He mentioned Not Normal."

"Yeah?"

"Said that one day... he'd make him pay."

"Keep well away from Paul."

"You're right." Charlie nodded. "Sure you don't want to go for a swim?"

"Not today. I've things to do."

"Me, too." Charlie looked relieved. "Well, call me when you want."

"Sure."

At the lake, I could do nothing but stare at the water.

"You weren't here yesterday," said a voice behind me.

I turned quickly to see Dakota smiling at me, and suddenly my world was okay again.

"I was here a couple of days ago. I couldn't find you."

"Can't find what doesn't want to be found," she replied, cryptically. "Anyway, we're both here now. Going for a swim?"

Before I could answer, she was stripping, her beautiful naked body emerging from the cocoon-like clothing.

"Stop gawking and strip!" she commanded. "C'mon!"

Away she went, running for the water, leaving me fumbling at my clothing.

In the water, she splashed while dunking me twice, laughing, throwing her head back with joy. She suddenly seemed like a kid, not the sophisticated woman I had imagined.

"Isn't this fun, Tommy?" Her eyes were smiling.

"Yes!" I shouted from the top of my voice.

I wanted this moment to last forever. I no longer cared about family or friends, life or any of those silly things.

After an hour of swimming about, she said, "Come on."

"You're going?" I was shattered.

"I've things to do." She began swimming towards land. "Hurry up and get out."

I quickly followed, feeling anger and disappointment boiling in me.

On dry land she scooped up her clothes, but didn't put them on.

"This way. Hurry," she said, smiling, running.

Quickly grabbing my clothes, I followed her into the wild and camouflaging grass, noticing for the first time the constellation of miniature horseshoe-shaped bruises on her buttocks. The marks were frightening to look at, but I couldn't take my eyes from them. It wasn't the first time I had seen marks like that.

Without warning, she pulled me down onto the grass, quickly rolling on top of me.

"Squeeze," she whispered, placing my hand on her left breast.

Hesitantly, I squeezed. Her breast was warm and small, like an egg after a hen goes to feed.

"Do you love me, Tommy?"

"Y... yes."

"Say you love me."

"I... I love you," I managed to say, throat sandpaper-dry.

Rolling off, she lay on her back, fully exposed.

"One day, when I think you're ready, I'll let you go

further than just touching my boobs."

"Further?" My voice was a croak.

"Yes, but things like that have to be earned. Do you understand?"

"Yes... but—"

"*Shhhhhhhh!*" She suddenly placed a finger firmly to my lips. Her eyes filled with terror. *"Someone's here, watching"*

The sweaty proximity of fear touched me for a second, making the hairs on the back of my neck tighten. I stopped breathing. Listening intently, I thought of Charlie. Had he followed me? Worse. Paul?

We lay there motionless for minutes, when suddenly there was heavy movement behind me. I wanted to get up and run, but without warning a hare burst through the long blades of grass, scampering over our naked bodies, scaring the shit clean out of me.

Dakota burst out laughing.

"Oh, Tommy! Your face!"

"Don't you talk! You were terrified."

Suddenly, she stood up and started dressing.

"Why're you going, Dakota? Angry at me poking fun at you?"

"Don't be silly." She kissed me on the lips. "I've got to go. My mum needs looking after. I can only get out for a couple of hours each day."

"Oh... I'm sorry." Suddenly I was filled with remorse, and embarrassed by my selfishness.

"It's okay. I've been looking after her for years."

"Don't... don't you have a dad?" I asked, regretting it the moment my big mouth opened.

"He... died... a long time ago."

"I'm sorry."

"Don't keep saying sorry." Her voice suddenly had an

25

edge. "It's not a word I like. It's weak."

"Can I ask you something?"

"What?"

"Promise you won't get mad."

"I don't believe in promises. They're always broken."

"Those... those marks, on your... butt..."

"Yes? What about them?" Her face was impassive, but her voice sounded cautious.

"What... what are they? They look like burn marks."

"If that's what they look like, then let them be just that," she said, pulling on her jeans, zipping them so loudly they sounded like a knife cutting into bone. "Are you finished questioning me?"

"Yes..." I replied sheepishly.

"Good." She made a movement to go.

"Can I walk you home?"

"No."

I felt my throat tightening. The thought of her leaving was killing me.

"When will I see you again?"

"When I decide. Okay?"

No, it wasn't okay. "Okay."

I stood watching her leave, thinking of those horrible marks. It would be much later before I'd discover their true meaning.

Over the following days, I got up early, running to the lake. Each time she didn't appear, misery wormed further into me.

I would never forget that early morning in bed, hearing Dad's voice filtering into my room. He was talking with Mum, but secretively, in hushed tones.

Sneaking out of my room, I hid on the landing, listening.

"Dreadful..." Mum kept repeating. "And you've no

26

idea who the young girl is?"

"Nothing yet. I've seen some terrible killings, Maura, but this was one of the most violent. She'd been raped, also, poor thing."

"Dear God..." From the stairway, I could see Mum's face cringe. Despite hearing the horrors of Dad's job every day, she had never managed to immunize her feelings. "People will be expecting you to catch this monster – and quickly."

Dad looked annoyed at Mum. "I've never rushed an investigation, just to calm people's fears. That's how mistakes are made. I won't be changing my ways just because of pressure."

"Of course not. I wouldn't expect you—"

Suddenly, they both looked up in my direction.

"Tommy? What the hell are you doing?" said Dad. He looked startled. "Were you listening in?"

"The girl, Dad? What... what did she look like?" I was slowly walking down the stairs.

"You shouldn't be listening—"

"What did she look like!"

"Tommy! Don't you dare shout at your father!"

Dad reached and touched Mum's hand. "It's okay, Maura. Sometimes it's good to shout." He was looking at me entirely different to the way Mum was. The cop in him was quickly kicking in. "Sit down and have breakfast, Tommy."

"I don't want breakfast. What... what did she look like?"

"She had dark hair, crapped page-boy style. Blue eyes. Her face was covered in—"

"Freckles."

Dad's face turned sombre. "Did you know this young girl, Son?"

"Her name's Dakota." I spoke of her in the present tense.

27

"Dakota? What's her second name?"

I couldn't answer. My voice was quivering, threatening to quit. Suddenly, tears were running down my face. Everything was spinning.

"It's okay, Son. It's okay," said Dad, leaving the table, edging towards me.

Of course it would never be okay. Not now. Not ever. And when I collapsed in front of him, that was the first blackout I had ever experienced. More would follow, all the way to adulthood.

That night, the nightmares started all over again. Only this time, Joey was joined by Dakota.

Over the next few days, details of Dakota's horrific murder and equally horrific life began to emerge. Her father abandoned her at the age of two, leaving her in the care of a mother hooked on drugs and alcohol. Margaret McKenzie – Dakota's mother – earned money for the drugs through prostitution. It soon became known that Dakota had been abused by some of her mother's clients.

I wasn't in the least bit surprised to hear that one of the clients had been Armstrong. My gut instinct had told me from the beginning that it had been Armstrong watching us in the long grass – not a frightened hare. It was little wonder Dakota had looked so terrified that day.

Over the next few days, the local newspapers made Dakota's brutal murder a *cause célèbre*, and relentless pressure was put on Dad to bring the perpetrator to justice…

Despite this pressure, it was three long weeks before he was able to accumulate enough evidence to finally arrest Armstrong. Forensics had matched his teeth with the marks on Dakota's buttocks. I shuddered when I overheard this piece of vile information.

It was only then, for me, that all the parts of the puzzle began falling into place. I had noticed the almost identical marks on Paul's buttocks, months ago as we skinny-dipped. When he caught me looking, he became angry, accusing me of being a 'homo'. We didn't speak to each other for almost a week, until he eventually calmed down, and we were able to laugh about it. His explanation for the marks was a raid on Mister Johnson apple trees, and a weak branch.

Lucky I landed on my ass rather than my head. I thought of his explanation and how feasible it sounded then.

Not now.

I believed Paul had been lured to Armstrong's trailer with the incentive of money – something Paul was always short of. That was how Paul knew all about Armstrong's comings and goings at the trailer – knew of the liquid in the cupboard, which I suspected had some sort of drug in it. That's why Paul insisted Charlie say he was thirsty, knowing Armstrong would go to the cupboard at the end of the trailer, and where Paul waited in the darkness to shoot. I shuddered at the thought of what happened to Paul, and now fully understood why he wanted to kill such an evil creature. It all made sense. Paul. Joey. Dakota. How many others?

As the weeks went by, Armstrong at first denied knowing Dakota, but finally admitted having what he called paid 'consensual' sex. The bite marks were part of the sexual act he enjoyed. She was sixteen, and there was no law against having sex with a consenting adult. Dad suspected the abuse of Dakota by Armstrong had started many years ago, but suspecting and proving were two different matters entirely.

After being held in the county jail for three months,

Armstrong was eventually released through lack of substantial evidence.

As days turned to weeks, Dakota's murder slipped down the list of priorities. The economy was in turmoil and people had more pressing things to think about such as jobs and livelihoods.

It was late December, when the town learned the news of Armstrong's body being found at his trailer. He had been shot, once in the head. I'll never forget the look of relief on Dad's face, when he told Mum the news.

"I only hoped he suffered," said Mum.

The newspapers held the same sentiments as Mum, but displayed them in a more professional manner, stating that sometimes justice takes a while, but once that while has come, it sure as hell takes. Someone said Christmas had come early for the town.

Three days after Armstrong's death I ran into Charlie.

"He did it, Tommy. Paul went and shot the perv. He really did it." Charlie looked terrified as well as excited.

"Don't talk about it. Understand? No one knows anything. If word gets out, he'll be arrested. You wouldn't want that, would you?"

"No... of course not. We... we're blood brothers, aren't we?"

"Forever, Charlie."

"Are... are you going to talk to Paul?"

"No. Best that we aren't seen together."

"Of course! I get it. They might be watching. Right?"

I nodded. "Best play it safe."

Charlie nodded, also, and then hit me with his news. "I'm leaving here, Tommy. Dad got a promotion. We're moving to Hastings."

Before I met Dakota, Charlie's news would have devastated me. But I had changed.

"That's great, Charlie."

"I'll probably come back, every now and again."

He was lying, of course. He had no intention of ever coming back. He was glad to be out of here, away from Paul, away from this town of monsters and bogeymen.

We shook hands, and I watched him walk away.

"Tom? Are you sure you're okay?" Belinda's voice brought me back from the abyss.

"Yes... really, love. I'm fine. Just need some fresh air. I'll be back in a minute."

I went out to the garden, taking the newspaper with me. A cool breeze swept through me, and I stood in it, feeling every pore of my hot body cooling down. The breeze immediately reminded me of the evening I dumped Paul's gun in the lake. When I went back to where he had hid it, I expected it to have been gone. But no, it was still there, in all its horrible glory, waiting for me.

When I went to Armstrong's trailer, I had no plan, only determination. That smile on his face was there, permanently etched like a guilty clown. When I shot him, he crumbled like a pile of dirty clothes.

I walked back to the lake, and threw the gun as far as I could, hoping it would rest where Joey's body had once been. Over the next few days, I waited to be arrested, but there was little interest shown by Dad or any of his colleagues.

Armstrong had so many enemies, it would have been impossible to even know where to begin, he told Mum. Besides, the town is saying Armstrong got what he deserved, and they don't want valuable resources being used up to find his killer or killers. Everyone is relieved.

Now, re-reading the newspaper article, I wondered how many would still be relieved?

31

DNA Evidence Reopens Murder Case
Newly discovered DNA proves that Norman Armstrong was not the killer of a young girl, Dakota McKenzie, over twenty years ago…

The story continued with the confession of a serial killer in prison wanting to clear his 'conscience' before being executed.

Armstrong's face kept staring out at me from the page. I could no longer look at it…

About the author

Sam Millar is a best-selling crime writer and playwright from Belfast, Northern Ireland, UK. He has won numerous literary awards and his books have all been critically praised. He is the recipient of the Aisling Award for Art and Culture, the Martin Healy Short Story Award, the Brian Moore Award for Short Stories and Cork Literary Review Writer's Competition. He has also had his work performed by the BBC, and published in over thirty literary journals throughout the world, including the USA, Australia, Europe and Africa.

Sam's work has appeared in best-selling anthologies, and he has written a number of crime novels. To find out more visit his website: www.millarcrime.com.

A Killer Week

Cathy Cole

A game of hide-and-seek

I like it when they beg. It adds a certain frisson, sending blood rushing through my veins, igniting my nerve endings, making them tingle. However, that is for later. For now I am content to watch and wait.

My latest Thing is Barbie-doll pretty, all flicked blonde hair and emaciated waist. She buys with careless abandon – a waft of a hand here, a glossy pout of lips there. Sales assistants fawn over her, rushing to her aid.

Rich bitches. They're all the same – flaunting their money, their bodies, themselves.

Today, I do a little 'flaunting' of my own, buying a pair of cool trainers, courtesy of my *good friend*, Bert, whose card and pin number I've borrowed. He won't miss the money, and if he does... tough. He owes me. He owes me, big time.

Thoughts of Bert agitate. I can feel my anger growing, swelling until it causes actual pain, stinging, like thousands of pinpricks on my skin. I can no longer contain myself. I have to have her.

Now.

Today.

I decide to take her in the car park. She starts at my approach, six-inch heels scraping cement as she turns. Now the moment is at hand I want to prolong it, to enjoy it. I duck behind a pillar, waiting.

"Who's there?" She peers into the darkness, voice unsteady with fear.

Her fear excites me, so I wait some more. It's a game of hide-and-seek. Soon I will be the only one in the game, and seeking is much more fun.

I step from the shadows, holding my hands up in apology. "Sorry, didn't mean to scare you. I'm looking for the exit to Baker Street?" I smile and see her eyes widen in appreciation.

"Oh, right." She giggles, becomes Barbie again. "I can, like, show you the way."

I lower my hands, allowing myself, and my smile, to relax. She is easy – like all the others.

When I step closer, close enough to inspect the open pores beneath the perfect make-up, she preens, tosses her fake curls. And when I take the stun gun from my shopping bag and jab it into her chest, she just stands there, looking at me with her big cow eyes asking, why?

Then she drops.

Pathetic!

I prise the keys from her unresponsive fingers, open the trunk and bundle her inside. Humming, I walk to the driver's side and get in. I leave the car park of the Odyssey using a ticket I obtained earlier – I had to pay a hefty fee, thanks to my Thing*'s* shopping marathon, which she, in return, will pay for later. The barrier lifts, and we're off.

I can't afford to draw attention to myself so I drive within the speed limit. No sense taking chances. Anticipation is almost as much fun as the kill.

Almost.

Burger to go

"Your daughter, Ally... is her first name Mohammad, by any chance?" Police Constable Sara Steward grinned at her boss as she left the car.

"Hilarious," Dickie said. He slammed the car door and stomped towards the cafe.

Sara followed, still in full flow. "Maybe I'll order

some *black-eyed* peas for lunch, what do you think?"

Dickie touched his swollen eye. Teaching his fifteen-year-old daughter self-defence had seemed like a good idea, telling her she had to return an expensive t-shirt she'd bought, in the middle of one of their bouts – not quite so inspired. "It was a lucky punch," he snapped, wishing he'd never opened his mouth in the first place. "But I've docked her pocket money, in case she tries to repeat it."

Sara giggled. "Let's hope all her punches are so lucky." Her voice lost its smile, "'cause there's a whole lot of ugly out there."

Dickie didn't need reminding. He'd spent many a sleepless nights worrying about it. "You going to flap your lips all day, Steward, or do you want something to eat?" He glanced at the specials, barking out his order, wondering how long they'd get for lunch today.

Sara was still learning. She perused the menu, debating the nutritional merits of fish versus gammon (plus or minus sauce), before placing her order.

"It's tough bringing up a teenager on your own," she said, as she sat down.

"And you would know?"

"I was a teenager myself – and not that long ago."

"You surprise me."

"I'm just saying if you ever need to talk…"

Dickie glared at her, more because he was tempted to take her up on her offer. Maybe she could explain why everything he said either made Ally furious or tearful – no in between. Whether it was a woman thing, or a teenage thing? Not that it mattered. He didn't understand either species. Times like these he missed Rachel the most.

Sara didn't push. "I get it," she said as the waitress appeared with his meal, "no personal stuff."

"Yup," Dickie muttered around a mouthful of meat,

35

"That's rule number two."

"Two? What's number one?"

Dickie grabbed his burger as their beepers sounded. "Order faster."

He let her drive while he finished his meal.

"Where to?" Sara asked.

"Odyssey Shopping Centre. Girl's gone missing. Name's, Krista Conwell."

"You think it might be The Cutter?" Sara tried to keep the excitement out of her voice.

Dickie hoped not. The Cutter, as the papers had dubbed him, left one hell of a messy crime scene. He forced down the last of his burger, wiping his hands on his trousers. "Even if it is, we're just there to do the grunt work," he warned, "before CID show up and take over."

Sara didn't care. This might be her first homicide and she was determined to experience as much of it as possible.

A job well done

I know where I'm going. I have a place picked out. It is beautiful, perfect, and, more importantly, secluded. It's a setting that lives in my childhood, a golden memory that stays with me because it is the only one I have. It is also the last time I saw my parents together, and my mother, Nancy, sober.

However, I don't think my Thing is going to enjoy it quite so much.

When I finish, I dump the body and abandon the car, key in the ignition, on the Ravenwell Estate. It doesn't last five minutes. It passes me, engine revving and radio blaring, doing sixty-five in a thirty zone. Before nightfall, I know it will be in pieces, neatly stowed in some back-street

36

garage, or burnt to a crisp on Wilson Common. Either way, there will be nothing to tie me to it. I congratulate myself on a job well done. To celebrate, I buy a large fish supper with the leftover money from good old *Bert*.

Nancy hovers while I eat, engulfing me in a fog of eau de vodka, until I feel like stabbing her with my knife. I need a place of my own – somewhere I can take my Thing*s*, play with them a while. The thought holds me. How cool would it be to keep them for a day or two, see the fear blossom over and over again.

My mind takes flight, making plans.

Later, in my room, I lie awake while an exquisite ache teases my nerve endings. I re-run the day in my mind. Apart from a few pieces of paper, my memories are the only thing I have to hold onto, because I take nothing from my Thing*s*. I watch *CSI*, I know trophies will get me caught, and I'm too smart for that.

The need rises, grows.

I need another Thing.

Soon.

Lust and Piles

She was no older than Ally.

Dickie swallowed back the greasy lump of burger reversing up his throat, and tried not to think about his daughter. It didn't help that the corpse was wearing the same, exorbitantly priced t-shirt they'd fought about that morning.

He wondered if Krista Conwell had fought with her parents before going out. The probability was that she had – something daft, unnecessary, normal, until you realised it could never be taken back.

"So young to have taken such a grown-up step," Sara said, sounding shaken, and not a little embarrassed by her original enthusiasm, "and in such a terrible way."

"Yeah, in a perfect world death would be confined to the elderly, and we would all die peacefully in our sleep, in our own beds." Dickie hawked, wanted to spit, but knew better at a crime scene. They hadn't made it as far as the abduction site, diverted here before they'd gone more than half a mile.

"What's first?" Sara had her notebook out, pen ready. Gone was the joker, the agony aunt, she was all business.

Patrol officers were doing the necessary, taping off the perimeter, holding people back. Dickie surveyed the scene. "Talk to our *audience*," he motioned to the crowd, "and get someone to take photos. I want names, ages… you know the drill."

Sara nodded, scribbled in her notebook. "Got it. Bastards usually stay to watch."

"Clarke will help." He waved to a uniformed officer, calling him over.

"Glad to see you're keeping the scene warm for me, O'Neil. And speaking of keeping me warm, Rachael says hi."

Dickie bit back a curse. He turned. Miles Henderson stood behind him, close enough to count the fillings in his teeth as he chomped on a huge wad of chewing gum. A younger man appeared at his side.

"You gonna' introduce us?" Miles gave Sara an appreciative look.

"Sara, meet Piles and…?"

"Guy," the other man said, eagerly holding out his hand, forestalling Miles' angry protest. "Guy Warner, nice to meet you."

"And you," Sara said.

Dickie gave an exasperated sigh, cleared his throat and looked pointedly at their clasped hands.

"Er… right. Sorry, Sarg." Sara flicked her notebook closed and backed away. "I'm gonna…" She waved a hand towards the crowd and scurried off.

"You dating, O'Neil?" Henderson gestured to Dickie's black eye, smirking.

"Why? You want more of my cast off's?" It was a cheap shot, and he knew he'd pay for it, but it still felt damn good.

Payback wasn't long coming.

"Time for CID to take over, kids, but don't worry, we got a juicy job for you." Henderson grinned at Guy, who was oblivious, still focused on Sara.

"I want every bit of CCTV footage at the abduction site – shopping centre, car park, surrounding area. Every car is to be accounted for – owners' names, addresses – plus I need details of all credit/bank transaction made there today, and I want them on my desk by end of shift. Think you can handle that... *Dick?*"

It was a mammoth task with an impossible deadline, but Dickie wouldn't give the bastard the satisfaction of complaining. "Piece of cake, Piles."

He looked on the bright side. Maybe he'd have time to nip home, get Ally's t-shirt and return it. The refund should pay for a couple of years of college, at least.

Famous at last

Her pain doesn't move me, her blood gives me no pause, rather, it excites me. I am pumped, ecstatic.

My latest Thing has been alive for two days and it's amazing what the human body can endure. I lower the drill. Maybe I should let her live? That way she can be a testament to my craft.

"Should 'a thought of that sooner," I mutter. She's seen my face. I could cut out her tongue, mash her brains a bit more, and even then she might still be able to identify me. I can't take the risk, plus, she won't stop screaming. She's unconscious, and I can still hear her irritating wails, begging for mercy.

God, she disgusts me. I want to hurt her some more, but she won't wake up. I pace the shed, my blood on fire, like a colony of ants marching under my skin. I'm running out of time. Bert isn't coming back, but someone will check in sooner or later.

"Wake up!" I kick her, hearing something break, not caring. She flops like a rag doll, blood trickling onto the wooden floor. The trickle eases, stops. I know what that means. God damn it. Why can't they last longer? Other killers make their Things last weeks, months, even years; my two days are nothing in comparison.

Frustrated, I pick up the paper I'd bought earlier. I was saving it, but now I need all the kicks I can get. I open it, savouring the moment, the sound of my Things' names as they roll off my tongue: "Kimberly, Natasha, Olivia, Evie," I trace their faces with my finger, "Chloe, Lucy, Krista." The list seems endless, even without today's offering.

I feel a thrill reading about the lives they lived, the hopes they had for the future. And each snippet, each little nuance of the pain I've caused them, and those around them, makes my heart leap and the ants cease their marching.

"I did that."

As much as I want to shout the words aloud, I'm glad there is no one but me and the Thing to hear.

I have to be careful.

After all, I have a reputation to protect now.

Getting nowhere – fast

It was four days since Krista Conwell had been abducted and murdered, and forty-eight hours after a second girl, Alicia Stinson, had gone missing. The faces and voices at the twice-daily update meetings became longer and louder as tempers flared and fear escalated. No one said it, but they all knew we weren't looking for a kidnap victim anymore.

Eight girls had gone missing in seven weeks. None had been found alive. As Alicia was the second girl taken this week it appeared the killer was accelerating his schedule.

"We should be out there doing something," Sara said, her frustration clear.

"Like what?" Dickie asked her. "Kicking in doors? A high-speed car chase or two? This isn't the movies. Policing is thankless grunt work, but it's the grunt work that solves cases, never forget that."

"As if I could," Sara muttered. Having checked and cleared every car owner in the shopping centre on the day of the murder, they were now working their way through the credit/bank card list. They were down to the last five.

"I like this guy," Dickie tapped a name near the end of the list. "Herbert Townsend. I have a copy of his driving licence here somewhere." He rummaged in his desk. "Ah, here it is. Says he's forty-two, 5ft 8, fifteen stone, bald. Lists his occupation as farmer, status, single."

"And him sounding like such a stud too."

Dickie grinned.

"Why do you like him?"

"Apart from his record, which shows he's done time for assaulting a minor – there was a whiff of sexual abuse, never proved – look at his credit history. He buys on line, gets everything delivered. He's used his bank card twice: when he got it three years ago, and the day before yesterday."

"Could 'a been stolen?"

"True, but that would still give us something. Mr Townsend is bound to know who had the opportunity to steal his card." Dickie scribbled the address on a piece of paper and grabbed his coat. "Either way, he's the best lead we have."

"Couldn't agree more," Henderson said behind him, plucking the paper from his hand. "Guy and I will take it from here."

There was nothing Dickie could do. Henderson was within his rights to take the lead. Still, it rankled.

"One less for us," Sara said, sounding cheerful. "We might actually get to clock off on time for once." She smiled at Guy, who winked as he left. "It's the weekend and I've got plans."

Dickie hadn't missed the little by-play. "You got a date?"

Sara blushed. "Maybe."

"Bit of advice – if he asks you to go back to his place, say no."

"Not that I'm admitting anything, but why not?"

"'Cause he lives with his mum." Dickie guffawed. "And three is definitely a crowd." He hunted through the file. "Got it."

"Got what?"

"There's a sister, Nancy Palmer, she lives just a few miles from Townsend with her kid. She might be worth a visit, if the rest don't pan out."

"Today?" Sara looked at her watch.

"Yes, today. You're the one who wanted to *do something*. This," Dickie held the paper aloft, "is doing something."

Sara wisely kept her mouth shut and went back to her list.

Mummy Dearest

I'm almost sorry to say goodbye to this Thing. Yes, she has irritated me with her constant screaming, but I've spent the longest time with her, learned so much.

For instance, she's afraid of the dark, of being alone. I never knew that… whatchamacallit… psychological pain, could be almost as much fun as physical pain. It adds a whole other level to my game.

I figure she deserves a little something in return.

Burying her on top of Bert might not be her idea of a reward, but at least she won't be alone.

"How's it feel to have a woman on top for a change, you old perv," I shout into the grave. Anger burns inside me, consumes me. I should have killed the bastard years ago, when he first touched me.

I rush to fill the grave, wanting him out of my sight, my mind. The sound of cars turning into the yard and doors slamming finally breaks my concentration. Who would be visiting Bert? Everyone hates the old buzzard.

I hear voices, loud, officious. My heart jumps. *It can't be.* I drop the shovel, running to the side of the barn, peeking out. Ahead are two cars, one unmarked, the other flashing blue and red lights.

How have they found me? I am at once incensed and fearful. This is my place. It isn't fair.

Mind in a whirl, I slip away. I go through the fields, keeping low as I run for home.

"Whas'a matter?" Nancy blocks my path, her breath sour, the stench of her unwashed body overpowering.

"Move!" I am breathless, frantic. Do the cops know about me? Will they be here next? How much time do I have?

"Don't speak to me like that." Nancy fumbles, grabs my arm.

"Why not?" It can't be over, not yet, not so soon. I think of my next Thing, refusing to give up. I have to have her. I have to finish what I started, but I have to hurry.

"Because I'm yer mum."

This strikes me as funny. "You don't know the meaning of the word, you old bat."

"Why you worthless lump of..."

"I don't have time for this." I push past her.

"Ungrateful little bastard." Voice slurring, spittle flying from her lips, Nancy pushes back.

That's when I lose it.

I hit her, striking out over and over. She sinks to her knees, arms raised to cover her head. It's easier to kick her in that position.

I kick her for a long time, until she shuts up – for good.

Bells will be ringing

"What's the deal with you and Henderson," Sara asked, as they drove towards Nancy Palmer's address. As they'd suspected, their other leads hadn't panned out; this was their last hope of finding Alicia Stinson.

"What happened to rule number two?"

"I'm guessing it went the same way as my plans for the weekend?"

She had a point, Dickie conceded, and figured he could give a little in return. "My ex, Rachael, ran off with Henderson, lives with him now."

"Ally's mother? She's still alive?" Sara sounded stunned, "I assumed…"

"See, this is why I have rules. Yes, she's alive. No, she doesn't want to see Ally, and no, I don't understand why. Anything else?"

Sara shook her head.

"Good. Is this the place?"

She checked her map. "Yup."

"Doesn't look like much." Dickie got out of the car.

Sara had to agree.

Together they approached the dilapidated house with its peeling paintwork and grimy windows. Dickie knocked the door. No answer. Just as he was about to knock again, his mobile rang. He looked at the display, tempted to ignore it when he saw Henderson's number.

"Your hunch was right, O'Neil."

The voice belonged to Guy, Henderson's partner. He sounded excited. "We've found two bodies. You got any background on Townsend we can use?"

"There's a sister," Dickie read out the address. "We're there now." He could hear Guy regaling this to Henderson, heard Henderson's muttered oath. He hid a smile and handed the phone to Sara. "It's for you."

He knocked the door again, knowing it was a lost cause. Empty houses had a distinctive echo. He turned the handle. The door opened. Motioning to Sara, he stepped inside.

The smell hit him first: decay, dirt, and the unmistakable odour of blood.

The body lay in the living room. Not Townsend, female. "Get Guy to call it in," he told Sara, who was still on the phone. She nodded, face ashen.

"Done." She handed the mobile back to him and together they searched the house. It was empty. When his phone rang again Dickie answered it straightaway. This had gone beyond his feud with Henderson.

"Yes?"

"What have you got?"

Dickie filled him in. "Body is female, best guess middle-aged. I figure Henderson's sister, but the face is too badly bashed in to be sure. Luckily, we have her prints from a drink/driving conviction a few years ago. What about you?"

"A male and female. No firm ID, but I'm guessing the female is Alicia Stinson. Clothing matches the description we have on file for what she was last seen wearing. The male is late thirties, early forties, bald... sound like anyone you know?"

"Damn! So Townsend's not our man?"

45

"Doesn't look like it."

"There's got to be a link. Townsend's dead, so is his sister, and her kid, Chris, is missing."

"Another kidnapping?"

"Could be, although it doesn't really fit the M.O." He heard Henderson groan, echoed it. When would this madness end?

"Get an alert out."

"Already done."

"Good. We'll be there ASAP."

Dickie closed the phone. In the distance he could hear sirens. Backup would be here soon.

"This is odd," Sara said.

"What?"

She held up a fistful of receipts. "They're all from the same place – Le Chic – that pricy shop in the Odyssey. It's just... Nancy Palmer doesn't strike me as a Le Chic kind of person."

"Me either."

"Could they belong to Chris?"

"Doubtful," Dickie looked around. "I just don't see them having that kind of cash."

"Then how did they get them?"

"Probably stole them."

"Why steal receipts, return receipts by the looks of it?"

An alarm sounded in Dickie's head. "Let me see." He grabbed the receipts, flicking through them. "Because these are the shop copies, they list the customer's name and address." Something else caught his attention. "Check out these dates. March 10th... that's when Kimberly Evans was abducted. March 17th... Natasha Bloomfield went missing that day. The 24th... Olivia Meriwether." He read them all; every receipt matched a missing girl. The last receipt was dated Monday of that week, and was for the return of an expensive t-shirt. A t-shirt just like the one he and Ally had fought over, the very same one that a shamed Ally had taken on herself to return before he could.

He dropped the receipts and sprinted for the door.

"Dickie?"

"Rule three," he yelled over his shoulder, "If I run, run!"

Revelations

Sara shouted directions into the radio, trying to make her voice heard over the roar of the engine. Dickie was oblivious, chanting a silent mantra, the words running together in his mind. *Please let me be on time. Pleaseletmebeontime.* Visions of the murdered girls, beaten and mutilated ran in a macabre loop in his head.

He took the corner to his house on two wheels; saw that Henderson had arrived before him. He screeched to a halt, bolting from the car, not waiting for Sara.

"Dic…"

"Don't," he told Henderson. "Don't even think about stopping me, that's my daughter in there."

"Wasn't intending to," Henderson said. "After all, she's Rachel's daughter too."

If Dickie had been stationary he would have punched Henderson there and then. As it was, he needed both arms to propel him up the driveway. "Nice of you to finally remember?"

"Always did," Henderson panted, "it's Rachael who doesn't." He paused, as if making up his mind. "She's in Arbour House," he said, naming a famous clinic, "has been for almost a year," he was breathing hard, trying to keep up with Dickie, "complete… mental… breakdown."

Dickie was stunned into immobility. "Why the fuck didn't you tell me? Ally at least deserved to know her mother didn't abandon her."

47

"She didn't want you to know." Henderson passed him. "Can we... talk... about... this... later?"

Dickie sprinted after him, overtaking him. He had his key out and in the lock by the time Henderson caught up.

From upstairs a scream rang out, high pitched and fearful.

Dickie made to dash up the stair, but Henderson held him back. "Could be a trap," he hissed.

"I don't give a fuck." Dickie shook him off. "I have to get to Ally."

"Get her killed, more like. Don't be an ass. We have surprise on our side, let's use it."

Much as he hated to admit it, Dickie knew Henderson was right. On silent feet, they climbed the stairs. As they crested the staircase Dickie felt his resolve crumble. Ahead lay a trail of blood, leading towards Ally's bedroom. Another scream rent the air. It didn't sound like Ally; then again, he'd never heard his daughter being butchered before.

Dickie forced himself to stay calm, kept his eyes focused on Ally's door. It didn't seem to be getting any closer, then, all of a sudden, they were there. He took a deep breath, trying to control his breathing as Henderson started the countdown. He held up his thumb.

One.

An index finger followed.

Two.

On the count of three they burst in to the room.

Dickie had tried to prepare himself, psyched himself up, but nothing could have prepared him for the sight that met his eyes.

Act 1, Scene 1

The next one was my undoing. I can admit that. I was too eager, rushing in without evaluating the situation properly – not something I am likely to repeat. However, in my

48

defence, there was no way I could know she was a copper's daughter, not so easily taken.

Cameras flash as I mount the steps to the courthouse, voices calling out.

"Why'd you do it, Chris?"

I don't reply. They could never understand.

I consider my options as the door to the courthouse moves closer. It's been two months since my capture. I've had plenty of time to work out my defence. I go straight into Act 1, Scene 1.

Doing my bidding, my green eyes well with tears; I drop my head, hunch my shoulders, acting contrite. I catch a few sympathetic glances.

Yup, tears might work. I'll have to try them on the judge. Maybe I'll get a Thing – Things like me, in the beginning anyway.

I catch sight of a familiar face in the crowd. The cop dad. He is surrounded by other coppers, their gazes cold and hard, but his eyes hold me. They are the closest thing I've found on this earth to what I carry in my heart. In their darkness I remember his daughter's fear, can almost taste her fury on my tongue. I touch the scars on my head, my neck, my arm, remembering what it felt like to lose that much blood, remembering how it felt to be on the other side.

I don't intend to be there again. Ever.

I am ushered through the vaulted doors and he is lost to sight. I smile. No, it is more a smirk, but I am too clever to let it be seen. It isn't so bad. I'll be out in a few years – they can't hold a ten-year-old much past that. And next time… well, I've learned my lesson. I'll be wiser in my choice. Police officers' daughters are out – unless, that is, I learn a bit more inside.

Dickie watched the killer disappear. At his side, Henderson patted his back in an awkward, avuncular manner.

49

"It's over."

"Yeah, we solved the case." Sara was glowing, and not just because her career had received a massive boost. "Didn't we, Hun"

"Did we ever, gorgeous." Guy swept her up in a kiss.

"Rule number four," Dickie barked.

The couple looked puzzled.

"He means: Get a fucking room," Henderson supplied.

The couple blushed.

"Will Ally be OK testifying?" Henderson asked, serious now.

"After beating the shit out of that little prick, what do you think?"

"Yeah, she's like her mum, got hidden depths."

Dickie was glad Rachael was doing well, would even entertain her getting in touch with Ally, if that's what Ally wanted, but Henderson was wrong. Ally was nothing like Rachael – there was nothing hidden about her.

He entered the courtroom, took his seat and stared at the killer. He wondered who Christina Palmer took after, and what else lay hidden beneath her innocent, childish facade.

About the author

Cathy Cole lives in Northern Ireland, with her husband and two sons, and a dog who thinks he's her third son. She loves writing – both short stories and novels – and is currently hard at work on her next novel.

No Privacy

Kirsty Ferry

Vanessa pushed her hands deep into her pockets and ducked her head into the biting wind. It was the thirty-first of October, and the chill of Halloween was seeping into the atmosphere. It was easy to imagine ghosts and witches, vampires and demons clawing at the veil that divided the living from the dead. The footpaths were deserted here and the street lamps gave off a sickly, sodium glow. Orange light pooled into the glossy black of the rain-soaked pavements, bleeding into the gutters and staining the edges of the scrubby bushes on the grassed over verges she passed. Jagged, wire fences towered above her, and here and there the shells of disused factories loomed up out of the shadows.

Vanessa walked alone looking neither left nor right. She was used to this area. She knew she just had to hurry through this estate and at the end of it, where the trunk road into the town met the lane she took to go home, she could relax.

Her home lay up the muddy lane, an end cottage in a row of three. Built for railway workers sometime within the last century, it was a shabby little place with one bedroom upstairs and a general purpose room downstairs. The bathroom was a crude extension to the house, leaning in from the yard, keyed into the old, blackened brickwork. The bathroom smelled of damp and the shower head rattled twice a day when the goods train hurtled past. The other cottages were derelict and nobody had any reason to come near them.

It was not so long ago that someone was murdered in the lane. The detectives who came out to see Vanessa suggested that she took extra care coming home at night and maybe spent a few nights away if she was worried. Vanessa had shaken her head and said, really, she was fine. One of the detectives had pressed a card into her hand anyway and told her to call him immediately, should she have any concerns. She thanked him and when he had left, she threw the card into the waste paper bin. Vanessa hurried down through the industrial estate, remembering the murdered man in the lane. She shuddered. He was so close to her house – things could have turned out very differently. When she reached the end of the road that led up her lane, she relaxed. The lane was deserted – a black tunnel beneath the trees. Branches reached across the space above her and intertwined themselves. In summer, walking home, she was dappled with green and golden light; in winter, the branches formed a stark, skeletal maze which let starlight and moonlight drip through their wizened fingers. Vanessa paused, and felt around in her pocket for her door key. This was part of her routine. She needed to have the key in her hand, ready to push into the lock and hear the welcoming click as the door creaked open. Swollen with dampness and hanging on old, rusting hinges, the door opened straight into the downstairs room, and once it was closed behind her, she knew she was safe.

Vanessa felt around for the key and could not find it. She wanted to close her fingers around the cold metal, her own private talisman. She dug deeper and deeper, pushing bitten fingernails into the lining of her pockets, pulling at loose threads and eventually her forefinger slipped into a hole which gaped open at the hem of her coat, just big enough for her key to fall through.

She swore and turned on her heels. She began to re-trace her steps along the road, back towards the artificial lights. She peered at the ground as she walked, hoping to see a sliver of metal; but she saw no key nestling in the gutter or balanced on the grid of a drain.

She squeezed through a gap in a wire mesh fence, which led onto an old car park. Burnt out vehicles used to be dumped here before the police barricaded the entrance. Vanessa knew how to wriggle past the mesh, and often walked through this car park. Other people had followed her tracks and the metal was now gnarled and twisted, sticking out ready to bite into your flesh as you pressed past it. Vanessa had already been in this area once tonight.

She stood in the concrete square and rummaged in her drawstring bag. She took a tiny pen-light out of it, and swept the beam in a golden arc across the wet ground. A glint caught her eye, and she knelt down to investigate further. It was a ring pull, lying in a dark, sticky puddle. She frowned and scanned further afield with her torch. There was what looked like a heap of old clothing nearby, and Vanessa shone her torch over towards it. Nothing. She sighed, and dropped the torch into her bag, tugging the strings closed. She took one last look at the car park, and gave a cursory glance to the heap of clothing. She headed back towards the gap in the fence.

Vanessa was just about to squeeze back out onto the street, when she heard the soft thud of footsteps echoing through the night. A figure was coming towards her. A large, bulky shape: a man. She stopped dead in her tracks. The footsteps grew louder and more hurried. Vanessa's heart began to thump loudly and she could hear it banging against her chest. The man came closer and she ducked behind the wall, out of his line of sight. She was thankful that the fog was rolling in; it wrapped its grey arms around her and hid her. She waited until the footsteps died away and she slipped out from behind the wall.

She followed him, the soft, leather soles of her boots

53

making no noise. Gradually, she began to catch up with him. She opened her bag, and fumbled around in it. Maybe the key was in there after all. The man stopped. He began reaching inside his coat pocket and brought out something small and rectangular – a mobile phone. He turned around, holding the phone to his ear and Vanessa pulled her hand out of her bag. She kept walking. The man started to walk in the direction he'd come from, back towards her.

Vanessa put her head down and hurried past him, not looking at him. The fog was perfect Halloween weather. Everyone wore masks and disguises at that time of year. The fog was Vanessa's disguise. She felt a little violated, seeing the man down here in what she deemed as 'her' estate. The only people that generally used this short cut were drunks or tramps – people of no consequence. Maybe a stranger would wander through, a stranger lost on the outskirts of the city and unsure of where they were. Occasionally, someone would stray down here that had the fond idea of redevelopment. They would stand on the path or in the middle of the road and look around, like this man had done. They would inexplicably shiver, and decide not to bother; the place had a strange atmosphere. Then they would turn and go, as this man had also done.

A few days before that, as rain had battered the window of his office, the detective who had pressed his card into Vanessa's hand looked through his case files. He fingered the file regarding the murder in the lane. He remembered the girl who had called in the murder.

"There's a dead man in the lane outside my house," she had said. Her voice was stilted and overly polite, as if she was unused to speaking to people.

"Let me take some details," Detective Inspector Harrison had said, pulling a pad of paper towards him and flipping it to a clean page. "First of all, what's your name?"

There was a beat, then a defensive,

"Why?"

Harrison stared at the telephone. "Because it would help me to know who I'm talking to. So I can take the details."

"Can't I just give you my address?" she had said. "Then you can just come and take him away."

"It doesn't work like that," Harrison said patiently. In his mind, he was thinking *another crackpot.* Out loud, he repeated, "Your name, please?"

"Vanessa."

"Thank you. And your surname?"

"You don't need that. I live at 1 Railway Cottages. Please come and take him away. He's starting to rot."

The phone went dead. Harrison held it as the dial tone hummed in his ear. Starting to rot? *For Chrissake, how long had the guy been there?* he wondered.

The team were there within the hour. As the girl had said, the body had started to decompose and the October storms had flayed the clothing on his body so the tattered rags waved in the air like so many banners. Or so many ragged fingers, depending on how you looked at it.

"Your guess, Tony?" Harrison said, standing beside the pathologist. Tony looked up at him.

"At least a week," he said screwing his face up in disgust. "It's in plain sight. How come she never reported it earlier?" Harrison shrugged, and pushed his hands deeper into his pockets.

"Any ID on the body?" Harrison asked.

"None. Wallet's gone. Nothing else on him. Just his keys."

Harrison nodded.

"Thanks, Tony," he said.

Crime Scene Investigators spent hours digging around the woods and the lane with no success. Whoever had done this had covered their tracks pretty well. Harrison noticed the girl watching them through the windows of her cottage. He beckoned to his partner, Detective Constable Rogers, then walked away from the crime scene and knocked on the front door. The girl cracked open the door and peered at the detective through the gap. Her gaze slid over his shoulder, taking in Rogers as well.

"May we come in?" Harrison asked. The girl paused for a moment then opened the door fully. Harrison stepped into the sparsely furnished cottage and Rogers squeezed in behind him. The men seemed to fill the room. Vanessa stared at them out of wide, cornflower blue eyes and Rogers smiled at her encouragingly. Harrison didn't waste any time on pleasantries.

"Why did you wait so long to report the body?" he asked her.

"I don't know. I don't think I realised he was dead. You sometimes get tramps and drunks around here – and the kids mess on near Halloween and leave all sorts lying around. Last year there was a chicken spiked on the fencepost over there. Dead cats and stuff. Roadkill. And they set fireworks off across in the woods for Guy Fawkes. I hate this time of year. I thought it was a pile of old clothes. Or a guy or something they'd left out to put on a bonfire. There was a mannequin hanging by a noose on my tree a while ago. I guess I just thought..." Then she burst into tears. "That poor man, that poor, poor man. What happened to him? If I'd heard anything... I could have stopped it..." Rogers apparently felt sorry for the girl.

"Don't worry, if you'd heard anything and gone out, you could have been the one lying there, not him," he said.

This brought fresh tears into the blue eyes and Vanessa sobbed and sobbed until the two detectives realised they would get nothing more out of her that night.

On Halloween night itself, the night she had lost her key, Vanessa reached the end of her street and broke into a run. She pounded up the lane, past her house and, flicking on her pen-light, scrambled through the broken door of the cottage on the far end of the row. She scraped her leg on the rough bricks that were stacked haphazardly in what used to be the hallway and tossed a plank of wood out of the way. She climbed over to the old fireplace and dislodged more bricks. She felt around inside the flue for her spare key. She poked her fingers into a hole and curled them around a shiny, new one. She pulled the key out and began to replace the bricks. She had realised it was a good hiding place quite some time ago. Very useful for her spare keys.

Vanessa heard a noise from the back room – a scraping and a thud as the old wooden door was pushed aside. She paused and listened. She heard a footstep. She dropped her key into her pocket and stared at the gap where the door should be. She flashed her light briefly towards the back of the room and she made out a black mass, a shadow of some description, moving towards the door. She backed away towards the hallway, and slipped out the front, her heart beating fast. She hoped whatever it was hadn't realised she was there. She had been truthful when she told the detectives she didn't like this time of year. Too many people gravitated to the woods and railway behind her house. There was supposed to be the ghost of a man who had hanged himself in the exact same cottage she had just left. His distraught girlfriend had allegedly thrown herself in front of a passing train when she discovered the body. Would-be ghost hunters loved Vanessa's street and Halloween was an exciting time of year for them. But Vanessa hated the disruption to her routine.

Vanessa slid the new key into her lock, and after the door had clicked shut, the figure in the derelict house came out of the shadows. Moonlight trickled through the old rafters, silhouetting the figure bent over the stack of bricks. Then it moved into the old living room, where it stood next to the fireplace.

The next day, All Saints Day, Vanessa was awoken by a knocking on her door. Her first reaction was annoyance. Nobody ever came down here. She blatantly ignored the knocks on the door at this time of year when groups of ghost hunters came to ask her for information and kids yelled "Trick or Treat!" through her letterbox, banging it again and again whilst whooping with laughter. The kids would run away across the railway tracks and she would be left simmering with anger, wishing Halloween was over and she could be left in peace once more.

Vanessa disregarded the knocking that morning as being more of the same. Then it became more persistent. A voice called through the letterbox,

"Open the door. This is the police." Vanessa's stomach flipped. "How *dare* they?" she hissed to the empty room and stormed down the stairs. "I never asked them to come back."

"Go away!" she shouted through the door at the person who was waiting outside. "This is private property."

"Come on Vanessa. Open up. Or would you prefer it if I called you Elizabeth Davies?" the voice answered.

"No!" Vanessa shrieked. She grabbed the closest thing to hand: a carving knife, which she raised in the air as she wrenched the door open.

Harrison was too quick for her. His hand flew out and he grabbed her wrist, smashing it off the door frame until she dropped the knife. He twisted her arm until she sank to her knees sobbing.

"Elizabeth Davies. You are under arrest for the murder of Joe Brooks and Alan Watson..." He continued to read Vanessa her rights as he charged her for murder.

Vanessa howled and sobbed and denied it. But Harrison knew better. It seemed that this abandoned industrial estate was Vanessa's own private hunting ground – her own space. Nobody came to check the car parks or industrial tanks buried deep in the earth. Security guards had long since stopped patrolling the area; CCTV was non-existent. Joe Brooks had apparently been taking a shortcut across the railway into the woods. If he'd stayed in the estate, then he might well have survived that night. He must never have seen the flash of silver that had taken his life.

After he was dead, or maybe even as she stabbed him, Vanessa must have lost her key – the key they had found next to the body. It was identical to the spare keys hidden behind the fireplace in the derelict cottage. Forensic analysis had confirmed that blood found on the bricks by the entrance to the old cottage and on the jagged wire fence near the car park belonged to Vanessa. The draw-string bag and knife had been safely hidden behind a loose brick in the fireplace of the dilapidated house; Harrison had found them as he had investigated the looser, cleaner bricks in the abandoned cottage the previous night. He had received a phone call from Rogers before that, as Rogers wandered through the estate trying to retrace the steps of Joe Brooks when he found the body of Alan Watson.

When the team had reached it, they'd found another door key, caught in the folds of the coat. The man had been stabbed – the same pattern as the body in the lane. Again, the door key had matched the one found on Joe Brooks.

Harrison had remembered Elizabeth's eyes more than anything. He was a rookie at the time, working on a murder case. The murder had taken place in an alleyway behind an old hotel, and Harrison had been haunted by a picture of the suspect for years. She had been a homeless girl, apparently sleeping in a corner of the abandoned foyer. Cornflower blue and innocent, those eyes had taken in everyone on the case, just as they had taken in Rogers. So Elizabeth Davies had escaped that time. But Vanessa, or Elizabeth, or whatever she chose to call herself now, wouldn't escape this time. Inspector Harrison would make sure of that.

About the author

Kirsty Ferry won the English Heritage/Belsay Hall National Creative Writing Competition in 2009 and has had short stories and articles published in magazines such as *People's Friend*, *Ghost Voices*, *Vintage Script* and *The Weekly News*. Short stories also appear in various anthologies including Bridge House's *Devils, Demons and Werewolves* and *Voices of Angels, The Best of Cafe Lit 2011*, *Whitby Abbey Pure Inspiration* and Wyvern Publications *Mertales* and *Fangtales*. 'Kirsty is also the author of the YA paranormal novel *The Memory of Snow*, now available on Amazon.

www.rosethornpress.co.uk

Perilous Truths

Jane Isaac

"Death is always personal, even when it's business," Kenny said. He leant back against an old crate and dug his hands into his pockets.

Rip, whose wide, frantic eyes were fixed on Kenny, started to shudder uncontrollably, as if the organs inside his body were individually jumping about in terror. His head darted from side to side. The shrieking yelps from beneath the duct tape that covered his mouth sounded more like a deserted puppy.

Mitch turned away, struggling to calm his quivering limbs, and took a deep breath. *Don't look at him. Stay composed.* The metallic stench of blood proved overwhelming. Fighting every one of his body's natural reactions, he exhaled slowly, and watched the puffs of white air disperse into the cool atmosphere as he strode over to the factory entrance.

Hauling a Jerry can to his side, he crossed back over the concrete floor, stepping over broken bits of wood, scraps of metal, broken shards of glass, his gaze still averted. He forced his mind to wonder, speculating what this disused factory unit had been used for, before it closed down. What had they made here?

The sound of Kenny gnashing his teeth, followed by a loud sigh, broke his abstraction. "Need a hand with that lad?"

"No." Mitch was taking too long, he knew that, delaying the inevitable.

He clenched his teeth and looked up defiantly, his hard eyes taking in Kenny's bulbous head, piercing, blue-grey eyes and tight mouth. There was no doubt he had worked out in his younger years, his number one hair cut and long black coat wouldn't be out of place on the 'doors' on a Saturday night. But lately the approach of middle age had covered the muscle with an expanding, soft layer of fat. Despite this, he was still a damn sight stronger than Mitch who, at eighteen years of age, was still developing the muscle that would make him a man.

Mitch walked up to the back of the chair where Rip was secured, hands tied behind his back, feet tied to each leg of the chair just above his ankles. The plastic garden ties were fixed one notch too tight, just enough to slowly sever the skin on Rip's small frame and make his fingers go white.

Mitch pushed his tousled brown hair out of his face as he bent down and undid the can, then started to pour. An overpowering stench of kerosene instantly filled the building. Rip's whole frame shook. A trickle of fluid ran down his trouser leg, puddling beneath his feet. Facing away from Kenny and fixing his wide eyes on a piece of broken metal on the floor, Mitch continued to douse Rip with the remaining oil, then stepped backwards. He pulled the box out of his pocket, struck the stalk of wood and flicked the match at the chair.

Mitch stood still, mesmerized for a split second by the sound of roaring flames and the muffled screams of his victim.

"Out!" shouted Kenny from the doorway. Mitch ran to the door feeling the unbearable heat eating into his skin.

It wasn't until he was out of the building that he noticed the flame on his arm. Kenny walloped his hefty hands against the flames, extinguishing them in an instant. Then the pain kicked in...

Twenty years later, Mitch looked at the burn mark on his forearm as he pulled the sun visor down to shield his eyes from the hot, summer sun. Over the years the arms had thickened, faint wrinkles appearing around his wrists, but the scar remained, like a map of Australia on his forearm – a constant reminder of a memory that had haunted him every day of his life since.

He pulled off the motorway at junction 16, the journey from North London barely taking him an hour, and slowed into a lay-by to text Annette. She would be busy getting their children ready for school, dropping them off around nine before she headed to the gym. Poor Annette. She had no idea. She thought he had gone to work in the city, just like any other day.

He pulled back his sleeve and checked the time. It read 8.30 am. Better give it a bit longer to make sure the area was completely deserted. He leant back and closed his eyes, allowing his mind to wander back…

Cal had offered Mitch the job when he was sixteen years of age. He guessed if there had been a mum around she would have flatly refused, seeing straight through the deception. But there was no mum, only him and his dad, and over the years he had seen how it all worked. Initially his dad was set against him joining the *'firm'*. "You've got brains son. You need to get a proper job. Make a good life for yourself." But Mitch had managed to wear him down, convincing him that it was only a temporary move to enable him to earn some cash, maybe get a motorbike – just to get him through college. Anyway, he would *only* be valeting cars. What harm could come of that?

Mitch had known Cal, the head man, since he was a toddler. Cal owned the Ruby Casino where his dad worked and had an air of wisdom about him, something usually enjoyed by men far senior to his years, and a brain for business. Self made, at forty he owned a string of properties, a car valet business, a launderette and two nail bars. But the drugs money Cal laundered was the real earner. The problem was that Cal recognised Mitch's abilities and intended to make the most of them, so much so that in a very short time, he was far more involved than he had ever intended to be – the lure of the money, its own brand of narcotic to fund his young, party lifestyle.

The day Mitch got his offer to study Media at University College London his dad had been so excited. Until they walked into the rear entrance of the Casino and saw Cal…

"Somebody looks like a cat with two tails. What lit your torch?" Cal said.

"Mitchell's had some fantastic news!" shouted his dad, slinging an arm around his son's shoulder, pride oozing from his pores.

"Well, let's have it?"

"He's going to University College London to do Media Studies." The atmosphere frosted over immediately.

"Ted," Cal frowned as he spoke, then held him arms out wide, "and leave all this. Why would he want to do that?"

"Come on, give the boy a chance," Ted said, his face tightening. "He's a clever lad."

"You know the rules, Ted. Nobody leaves." A mean smile spread across his face.

"He's only cleaning cars. And you agreed it was only ever temporary. Come on, this is his real chance. You know he wants to produce music."

Cal shot Mitch a beguiling glance. "And I want to make a living. I'm sorry, Ted. We've been together a long time and you mean a lot to me, but the boy's really shown his worth over the past two years. He's too valuable. He knows too much." He nodded his head towards Mitch. "I'll make sure he earns a good living here."

Mitch watched his dad's face cloud over as if he were watching his dreams of a better life for his son slipping through his fingers. "Can we talk about this? Alone?"

Cal's expression hardened. "Sure." They marched into Cal's office together.

When they emerged, over half an hour later, Ted's face was ghostlike. "We're going home," he said to his son, a conciliatory note to his voice.

"What about Uni?"

"We'll talk at home." They had walked back home in silence that evening. His dad opened two cans of Guinness and they sat at the table as he gave him the news. He could go to university, but he had to do Cal a favour first. A favour so special, that it would show Cal how committed he was to the 'firm', and how determined he was to keep his mouth shut. Then he could have out. For now...

The sound of a car door slamming shut jolted Mitch's eyes open. As he watched the driver of the car parked in front move to the rear of his vehicle, open his boot, and rummage through the contents, he sighed. How could this come back to haunt him now, after twenty years? The dashboard clock read 9.00 am. Time to go. He shuffled forward and started the engine.

Mitch reached his destination, an area named Durton, in less than ten minutes. He bit his lip as he pulled into St Clifford Park, which was built close enough to the

65

town's station to encourage the influx of London overspill to the Midlands, lured by country living and a one hour commute. It was the kind of modern housing estate which was as quiet as a graveyard during the day and became alive after dark, as if it were inhabited by a community of vampires.

He parked his car on the edge of the estate and glanced around nervously, pulling the hood of his sweat top up, before walking for 10 minutes past numerous houses of similar design, shoe horned into position with postage stamp gardens. When he finally reached his destination, he snuck around the back, slipping in through an unlocked gate. Forcing the back door proved easier than he thought and he dropped his holdall down on the kitchen floor and looked around.

The sink in the small fitted kitchen was full of dirty dishes, cutlery and used coffee mugs. A strong smell of stale tomato ketchup hung in the air. The room led directly into a lounge which housed an oversized old sofa at one end under the window, and a dining room table at the other. He followed through the door that led out into the hallway and checked upstairs to make sure it was empty before he got to work; then sat down on the sofa, and waited.

He reached into a pocket and adjusted the position of *the letter*; the same letter that had arrived seven days previously. Strangely, it wasn't really a surprise, almost a relief after looking over his shoulder for so many years. But still, it had shaken him. And he couldn't help wondering: why now?

He remembered how he had flown out to Spain the very next day to see his dad, who had retired out there when Cal passed away almost two years before. His dad had read the letter aloud, astounded.

66

"I have evidence to link you to the Rip Bane Murder. You know what I'm talking about. If you don't transfer £25,000 to the bank account below within the next 14 days, I will send my evidence to the police. The camera never lies…"

Ted was silent for a moment, deep in thought. Then he narrowed his eyes and pressed his lips together. "Kenny…"

"No. It couldn't possibly be!" Mitch had replied. "He was there with me that night. He has just as much to lose."

"Exactly."

"What do you mean, 'exactly'? And why now? Why not ten years ago, or fifteen?"

"Think about it. You're established in your career, at the top of your game. You're comfortable financially, with a wife, kids, good lifestyle."

They had sat in silence for some time before Ted continued, "I'm surprised at him, he was always so loyal. But now that Cal's gone, the threat of any repercussion is limited. He's thought this one through; the timing's so dangerous, it's clever."

Mitch drained the whisky from his glass. "So, what do I do?"

"Maybe, he's bluffing," Ted said finally, shaking his head as if he was still churning it all over.

"What makes you say that?"

"What on earth could he have? You were both supplied with concrete alibis by Hartel's for Rip Bane's murder, and the jeweller that gave you that alibi died a year ago. Kenny certainly couldn't have anything that could *only* expose you."

"The camera never lies," Mitch read. "Is that supposed to be some sort of clue?"

67

Ted was quiet for a moment, mulling it over. "Camera footage, maybe? There couldn't be any at the factory unit, it was burnt out. No, he's bluffing," he repeated, nodding his head now with an air of certainty.

"Well, bluffing or not. I'm going to have to deal with it before it gets out of hand." Mitch shuddered at the sound of his own words.

"True enough, son. But deal with it yourself. Make sure no one else is involved. We don't want this escalating."

Mitch heard the hum of a car engine outside. He shifted away from the window and made his way out into the hallway, pulling the knife from its sheath in his pocket, and stood behind the door.

The key was inserted, the door clicked open. Mitch's heart was pounding so fast he had to grit his teeth to control his breathing. Adrenaline soared through his veins. He pounced, throwing the pillowcase over Kenny's head, tightening it around his jugular and kicking the legs from beneath. It was easier than he imagined. He reached into his pocket for the plastic garden ties and strapped Kenny's wrists together, tightening them until his body flinched with pain.

"Walk slowly into the lounge," Mitch said once he'd finished.

He followed, keeping a firm hold on the material around Kenny's neck, until they reached the wooden dining room chair placed in the middle of the floor. Mitch shoved Kenny onto a chair and quickly fixed two more garden ties, tying each leg, just above the ankle, to the front legs of the chair. Finally, satisfied with his work, he stood back and removed the pillowcase.

Kenny's appearance had changed dramatically in the twenty years they had been apart: he was an old man now, thin strands of grey hair swept back over his balding head, his face was blotched with age spots, his cheeks sunken, lips thin. Any muscle was now soft and hanging from his frame. Only his steely reserve appeared to remain intact.

"You came." He managed a weak smile.

"I'm disappointed in you, Kenny," Mitch replied, panting slightly. Surprised at his own breathlessness he raised his head slightly, tilting it to one side. "If you were expecting me, then you didn't prepare well."

"I didn't think you got your hands dirty these days." What did he mean *these* days? He had only done it once, and once was more than enough. "Look at you," Kenny continued mockingly, "shaking like a leaf after rolling over an old man. You were never cut out for this work, were you?"

Mitch looked down, suddenly noticing the nervous tick in his left leg shaking violently from the surge of adrenalin. He took a deep, angry breath. "What is the meaning of this letter?" he said through clenched teeth. As he spoke he pulled the envelope out of his pocket and flicked it across the room. Kenny shrugged, then flinched as the paper clipped the side of his head.

"Is that it? No explanation?" Kenny shrugged again and Mitch couldn't resist the urge to kick him in the shin, hard. He jumped violently, but made no sound.

"Why now?"

Kenny looked up at him, his teeth clenched, nostrils flared. "Why do you think? You have it all you smarmy git."

"So you thought you'd blackmail me, get your hands on some of my hard earned money?" He snorted. "What have you got that is so damning?"

"Camera footage," Kenny replied with hard, resentful eyes.

"The warehouse burnt down. How can you have footage?" Mitch laughed out loud and turned to look out of the window at the willow tree across the road, its young branches shifting in the summer breeze, feeling a mixture of relief and incredulity. This was ridiculous.

"Footage that refutes your alibi."

He snapped back. "What do you mean?"

"You surely haven't forgotten the alibi Cal fixed for us? We were collecting his watch from Hartel Jewellers in Kelling that evening, a private arrangement. He chose it especially, being thirty miles from the warehouse. The shop manager even pulled us out of a line up to identify us."

"So?"

"There was a hidden camera. The jeweller kept it as insurance. It records date and time, and shows that two men did call around at 8 pm that evening, but those two men weren't us. Nobody knew about it – not Cal, not the police, not anyone."

"So, why now?"

"He came to me eighteen months ago, just after Cal died. He wanted some cash and offered to sell it to me. I figured it's only fair you should pay your share."

Mitch again laughed out loud, but his eyes were hard. "You can't tell me you paid £25,000 for it!" he replied scornfully. Kenny stared at him and said nothing. A muscle flexed in his jaw. "And what good is it anyway?" Mitch asked. "Even if it does refute our alibi, they'll need more evidence than that to pot us for murder."

"Aren't you forgetting something?" Kenny asked, his gruff voice grating. Mitch didn't reply, just stared at him. "DNA?"

70

Mitch frowned at him. "They didn't have DNA evidence in those days."

"No, but they do now. And he bloodied your nose in the struggle, didn't he? You bled all over him."

"So?"

"So. You hung his jacket up outside. Your blood will be on that jacket. *Your* DNA. All the police need is a suspicion of a phoney alibi and they'll take a DNA sample and you'll be banged to rights." Mitch turned away and shut his eyes. That part was true. This was a drugs killing to warn off a rival gang and Cal had demanded that they leave a trophy – Rip's infamous jacket hanging nearby, so there could be no doubt. And he *had* bled in the tussle. But would there still be his DNA on the jacket now?

He eyes switched back to Kenny. "And so will you."

"I don't think so." Kenny looked away, his voice smug now. "You forget. I've done several stretches over the years. I've given my DNA sample. It automatically goes into a police computer where it compares you to unsolved cases, but they haven't linked me to anything."

"I don't believe you."

"Believe what you like. The only reason the cold case review team haven't been knocking on your door is because you don't have a criminal record, which means they've never taken your DNA."

Mitch shook his head. "So, where is the tape?"

Kenny's eyes widened. "You think I'm gonna tell you that?" He watched as Mitchell scanned the room. "It's not here. I'm not that stupid."

"How do I know that you're telling the truth?"

"You don't. You'll just have to wait and find out."

Mitch stared back at him. He really wanted to wipe

71

that mean smile off Kenny's face. He had never liked him. But now he hated him more than he had ever hated anything in his life. He looked away and took a deep breath, remembering his dad's words. *"Don't lose your temper son. Kenny was in the game for a long time. If he does have anything, he may well have made provisions if anything suddenly happens to him; an insurance policy..."*

Mitch exhaled slowly and turned back to face his adversary. "Maybe you and I can help each other?" He spoke slowly, carefully and watched as Kenny looked up. He had his attention. "Say I believe you," he continued calmly. "How do I know that £25,000 will silence you forever? Even if you give me the tape, how do I know that you don't have a copy?"

"You don't know that either. You'll just have to trust me."

"How about we consider another arrangement?" Mitch said, his mind racing through the options.

"What do you mean?"

"Monthly instalments." He pushed the corners of his mouth down briefly. "Call it a pension plan. I buy your silence. That way it'll be in both our interests for you to keep your mouth shut."

"How much?"

"£100 per month."

Kenny sniffed. "You must be joking. £500."

"No way, if you live for another twenty years that's £120,000. "£150.""

"Be reasonable. I'm an old man."

"£200. That way, if you live for twenty-one years or more you'll have made over £50,000. That's my final offer."

Kenny tilted his head to one side and pressed his lips

together, stretching his face. He nodded slowly. "Fair enough. I'd shake your hand but I'm indisposed..."

Four months later Mitch awoke with sweat soaking his brow. His heart was palpitating again and he lay still for a moment, breathing deeply to control the chest pains. He was living off his nerves: every time the phone rang, he jumped, jolting every organ in his body; every time he went out, he looked over his shoulder. Sleep provided no respite, the nightmares more horrific that the waking memories.

For three months the payments had been transacted successfully. He paid via his dad who surreptitiously organised a payment into Kenny's bank account from a friend's account in the UK; nothing that could link the payment directly with him. But Mitch knew it couldn't go on forever. Sooner or later Annette would notice their bank accounts were down, would start asking questions.

He cast his mind back. Travelling back up to Durton had not been a problem; he'd told Annette he was away on an overnight conference. He'd stayed at the Travel Lodge and paid in cash. Even getting into Kenny's house quietly and quickly in the early hours, using the key he had taken from his last visit, had proved simple. Kenny had been sound asleep when he had placed the spare pillow over his head. He'd barely struggled at all. He remembered feeling almost pleased that there would be no defensive bruising. It would just be another old man, dying in his sleep. That was two weeks ago. And that was when the nightmares really began.

Mitch had read that assassins often vomit violently after their first killing. Then, as time goes on they harden to it, numbing their own emotional reactions; it became

73

just a job. Whether it was due to the twenty year time lapse, or just down to his weak personality he wasn't sure but, for him, what followed the second killing was even worse than the first. This was living hell. He was a killer. He had murdered two men. He could explain the first killing, attempt to justify it through his youth and the situation he had found himself in. But he couldn't use that excuse this time. He was a grown adult, with responsibilities, a family, children.

He turned his head and could just about make out the contours of Annette's gentle face which lay next to him in the darkness. He watched the regular rise and fall of her chest beneath the bedclothes. She looked calm and peaceful. Slowly, he eased himself out of the bed, grabbed his robe and wrapped it around his cold shoulders.

The clock in the kitchen read 2 am. He sighed and flicked the switch on the kettle before opening his laptop. Work offered a brief reprieve. He decided to work himself to exhaustion, when dreamless sleep would hopefully be inevitable.

By the time he had made a black coffee and settled himself at the table, rolling his tired shoulders in a circular movement in an effort to release the knots that had gathered at the base of his neck and across his shoulders, there were new email messages on the screen.

The first appeared to be from his dad, with a new email address, entitled 'Forthcoming Arrangements'. Good, he had finally set up his new computer. About time. He clicked it open.

Confusion turned to fear as an icy chill ran down his spine, gathering momentum as he noticed the attachment entitled 'Alibi', dated that fateful morning, two weeks previous. *That's the problem with the internet; it brings*

74

trouble into your home. He glanced over his shoulder as he opened it.

What Mitch saw on the screen made his blood run cold and breathing halt. He watched himself talking to Kenny tied to a chair in the middle of a room, listened to his voice as he negotiated payments. The chest pains returned, searing through his torso as he closed the attachment and scrolled down.

The message was brief:

'The price just went up to £50,000.'

About the author

Jane Isaac studied creative writing at the London School of Journalism. Her debut psychological crime thriller, *An Unfamiliar Murder*, was released in February 2012 by Rainstorm Press.

Jane lives in rural Northamptonshire with her husband, daughter and dog, Bollo. When she is not writing she loves to travel and believes life should be an adventure.

Jane loves to hear from readers and writers. Visit her website at www.janeisaac.co.uk or follow her on Twitter: *@JaneIsaacAuthor*, or Facebook: *Jane Isaac Author*.

A Routine Job

Don Nixon

I hadn't been given all the background. I prefer it that way. Then you can keep it strictly professional and impersonal. Nevertheless, I sensed there was something special about this assignment. Albie had seemed a little hesitant at the briefing. Some people say Albie uses me but for the moment I don't mind. Through Albie I make the contacts that will come in handy later on. Anyway, where at my age would I pull in the money I do?

I spotted him immediately at the far end of the café. I didn't need the photograph Albie had given me. I watched him from the doorway as he sipped a mug of tea. Among the brightly dressed tourists in their colourful tee shirts and designer jeans, he stood out like a shrivelled old crow perched amid a flock of gaudy chattering parakeets. He'd probably worn the black serge suit at his trial. It was at least twenty years since jackets had such narrow lapels and the pleated trousers had long gone out of fashion. He stared straight ahead ignoring the bustle around him. I've seen that abstracted self-contained look before with lifers. It goes with the parchment pallor that eats into the skin like leprosy during a long stretch inside. Some cons never lose it completely, especially the ones who have done most of their bird in high security.

I made my way to his table and pulled up a plastic chair. I brushed away crumbs lying on the seat and tried to guess the origin of the greying stain on the fabric. I hate a mess and my pin stripe was new for my appearance in court later that afternoon. I wiped the table top with a paper serviette and walked over to the bin. It was crawling with flies. Disgusting.

He gave a brief nod then looked ahead again. I controlled my irritation. I was used to undivided attention. I suppose it was part of his strategy for survival inside aiming for the dominant position, forcing me to speak first. It's a game a lot of old cons play. A compulsion to stake out territory, to be the alpha male in the prison wing.

But I could keep silent for as long as it took. Nowadays nobody plays games with me. I've been tutored by experts. Finally he sighed and gave in, forced a thin smile that didn't reach his eyes and spoke.

"Albie said you'd be on time. Said you were an anal little sod. I watched you fold that serviette into neat squares before you threw it in the bin. I bet if you were inside you'd tidy your bunk immediately you got up and then wash your hands at least three times. I once had a cellmate like you. Nearly drove me mad with his fussy ways. Obsessive like you. Yes definitely an anal type and believe me I know what I'm talking about. I've been gone over by the best shrinks in the system. I know all the jargon."

His voice was a low monotone and husky. I noticed he took deep breaths as if they were part of a regular health regime, painstakingly learnt. I could smell his suit – a whiff of camphor, probably from years in storage. I hid my sudden spurt of annoyance. Anal! It was what my ex girlfriend used to say before she walked out on me. I can't understand it. Why should being neat and tidy with everything kept in it proper place be something to be sneered at? When my mother was alive, the house was kept spotless and I always had three freshly ironed shirts each day.

"Albie's a good client," I said. "Puts a lot of work my way so I do exactly as he says. He doesn't like to be messed around. He said twelve noon and that's exactly what it is now."

"Very wise of you. Nobody ever crossed Albie in my day either. Can be a dangerous lad our Albie."

He still had his teeth but they were yellow stained with nicotine. Several cigarette ends were crushed in the ashtray, which no doubt accounted for the huskiness and laboured breathing. He looked at me and grinned.

"He knows where too many of the bodies are buried. Eh?"

He paused waiting for my reaction.

"In a manner of speaking that is," he added and laughed.

I kept my expression neutral and didn't respond. There was no "in a manner of speaking" about it. Albie did know where many of the bodies were buried. And so did I. Indeed I'd helped to plant some of them and I guessed in his time this old man had done the same. The construction industry had been booming in the eighties when this old guy was around. It was easy then I'm told when you had dodgy contractors in your pocket. They say that the M25 is not only the biggest car park in Europe but it's also the biggest cemetery for villains. Close to the centre of town, excavating going on all the time and a ready supply of concrete on the spot. Now with the recession and the collapse of the building trade, getting rid of unwanted clients demands more imagination.

Not many know of the work I do except those who matter and I make sure the bosses of the other firms north of the river know I'm not just some fresh faced young brief Albie has put through university. They give me respect when I have to work in North London outside our own manor. I'm gradually building a reputation. I aim to have my own firm soon. It all comes down to respect. Without respect, you don't last long in this game.

"You're a bit young for this job," he said and peered closely at my face. "I suppose Albie has brought you up to speed. Told you what I want."

I shook my head.

"No. Just that I was to do whatever you asked. He wasn't too pleased when you didn't tell him where you were living when you were released," I added. "And to be honest he didn't sound all that interested in the job. I got the impression it was a bit of a favour for old times' sake. He said it was routine. A routine job."

He frowned. I noticed his fists had clenched. Definitely a short fuse merchant but he was weak now. He must have been living off his old reputation inside for years. He managed a fleeting smile.

"Well you're right about the old times bit. We go back a long way. So he told you nothing?"

"Only that you needed a reliable brief who knows the street."

A child at the next table started to cry. The parents did nothing to shut the kid up. He winced.

"Bloody kids! Let's get out of here. Too noisy. I've been out three days and already I'm missing the quiet. You may not believe me but there's something peaceful about a cell when you get used to it."

I didn't believe him. I'd visited a few clients inside and after the smell of piss, floor polish and disinfectant that seems to seep into the walls along the wings even in the newest prisons, the next thing you notice is the constant background noise. I'm told Broadmoor is quieter but he'd only been there at the start of his sentence before they realised the madness was an act and he'd soon been shunted into a mainstream Category A.

I followed him outside and we found a bench on Tower Hill. Below, a queue snaked back to the river from

79

the entrance of the Tower. He looked around and shook his head.

"A lot of poor buggers ended up down there. I got interested in History in prison. Did an Open University degree to pass the time. Loved the Tudors. I understand these people. Dog eat dog and no prisoners taken. Albie would make a good Tudor monarch. Likes to be flash and obviously in control. I'm more of a Thomas Cromwell myself, A fixer."

He gave a mirthless grin.

"Mind you that didn't stop Thomas getting the axe in the end. Occupational hazard."

He pointed to Tower Hill.

"Over there is where the scaffold stood. A lot of them got topped there. Thomas Cromwell, More, Fisher, Essex. The women got the chop down there, inside on Tower Green. They sent for a French executioner with a sword for Ann Boleyn. Took it off in one swipe when she was looking the other way. The others got the axe. Did you know that Catherine Howard practised putting her head on the block the night before? That's style for you. I've always liked a bit of style. At least it was a quick death."

He sighed.

"You know the first few years inside I thought I'd rather have been topped. It would have been quick not like the long years of a life sentence. And till I got transferred from Broadmoor, you were just a specimen for any young shrink to practise on. Mind you it was amusing for a while to invent stuff for them to use in their PhD theses. I turned my so called child abuse into an art form in my descriptions. They use to queue up to get me on the couch. It's a wonder, my poor old Dad isn't still spinning in his grave at the things I pretended he got up to."

He laughed.

"Amazing how gullible some of these academics are. But in the end I went too far and a bright old shrink got me sussed out and then it was back to mainstream porridge. After that it was years of boredom in one high security stir after another."

His voice hardened.

"But I stuck it out. Lucky for me the current Home Secretary is a bleeding hearts Guardian reader and they need the space now with the prisons packed out. I know all the shrink shtick backwards. I can turn on the rehabilitation spiel in my sleep. I used to give lessons to mates in doing remorse and teaching the right body language for the Parole Board. Kept me in snout. But now I'm out and I've still got a few years left. I intend to make the most of them."

His lips tightened and the stained yellow teeth gleamed. I thought of a mangy old dog that was still capable of giving a nasty bite.

"Pity most of the ones who set me up are dead by now. I'd have enjoyed a bit of revenge. But there's still time for some payback for the ones who are left.

He began to cough. The wheezing went on for some time. I thought of emphysema. Too many fags. He sounded like my mother in the hospice. Lying in a hospital bed, choking under an oxygen mask. I tried to block the image from my mind. The wounds were still raw.

"What made you change your mind?" I was curious. "Why didn't you top yourself? There must have been plenty of opportunities. The screws wouldn't have been too bothered trying to stop you. Probably glad to be rid of you."

He peered at me closely. A trickle of spittle lurked at each corner of his mouth. He laughed.

"You're a cool young bugger. Not much sympathy

from you is there? I can see why you get on with Albie. In answer to your question – unfinished business."

I waited. Most cons want to talk. But I've found that they often like to be a bit mysterious. It makes them think that they are in control. They'll hold back, like to make you sweat a bit. But I could be patient. This was an important job.

"I don't care how you get it," Albie had said earlier that morning, "but I want that information."

Usually Albie keeps his cool but this time he was edgy. I wondered again if there was more to the job than he was telling me.

The old man coughed and wiped the phlegm from his mouth. I looked away. He was disgusting. I wondered how long the quacks had given him. He lit another cigarette. The breeze blew the smoke in my face and I fanned it away. He grinned as I spluttered.

"I expected Albie to come himself and show a bit of respect but now you are here you may as well tell me about yourself. I need to know who I'm dealing with. Whether to trust you."

He raised his eyebrows.

"You could be a young copper's nark on the make for all I know. Most briefs are in and out of bed with the police when it suits them."

I shrugged. Albie had said I had to humour him.

"Not much to tell. I grew up in Canning Town. My mother was left on her own when my dad scarpered with another woman when I was very little. I don't remember him and anyway Albie told me he died years ago. Albie looked after us. My dad worked for him in the old days and Albie always had a soft spot for my mother. I did well at school so he put me through uni and I did my lawyer training after it. Then he gave me a job. Albie has been like a father to me. I owe him a lot."

He nodded.

"It figures. Albie always likes to look after his own. Like Marlon Brando in that Mafia film."

"The Godfather."

"Yes. He liked to see himself as a sort of East End Godfather. Though perhaps 'Fairy Godmother' might be a better fit given his tastes. Does he still like you to kiss his hand when you meet him like they do in the film? He was a great one for the gangster movies in the old days. Think he fancied himself as a Mafia Don. Does he still wear a cream suit?"

He grinned and there was a snide edge to his tone. I got the impression that the two weren't as close as Albie had implied when he'd briefed me. I didn't respond. Albie never makes a secret of the fact that he swings both ways. I've noticed that some of the gang bosses are bi or gay like that Kray twin, though not the small fry who make a big thing about being macho and straight. Protest a bit too much some of them. Who cares now? But it was probably different twenty odd years ago. Closet doors then were kept firmly shut and some of the foot soldiers still have an old East End approach to where sex is concerned. Strictly missionary position stuff. Keep your vest on and the light out.

I kept my expression impassive. When he saw no response was forthcoming, he shrugged and went on a different tack.

"Is your mother still alive?"

"She died last year."

He paused for a moment and seemed unsure what to say. He held up one hand and gave a slight nod.

"I'm sorry," he said finally. "What was her name? I might have come across her back then. Your father too,"

83

he added, "if he was one of the firm."

I didn't want to speak about my mother. I'd managed to shut out those last dreadful days at the hospice but Albie had said it was important to get him to talk. It seemed this was the only way to open him up.

"Her name was Sandra Bates," I said slowly. "My dad's name was Bernie Flaxton. They weren't married. That's why I am Gordon Bates."

He frowned.

"I don't recall him but I think I do remember your mum, Gordon. A pretty blonde girl with one of those big beehive hairdos. Good legs too. All the guys were after her. A bit like Barbara Windsor in those *Carry On* films but with a lot more class.

"Definitely a lot more class," I agreed.

He thought for a moment then put out his hand. His grip was weak and I could feel brittle bones under the skin.

"You'll do sonny," he said.

In the taxi he explained.

"Since I got out I've been followed. It may be the filth. I don't know. Or it could be someone from the old days. They know the stash was never recovered. That's why I arranged the meet with you at the café. I chose the café for old times' sake. It's out of the way. It was where Albie and I planned some of the jobs in the early days. I made sure I wasn't tailed here. It's important nobody sees you with me."

"Why's that?"

"If they don't know about you, then they won't be on your arse when you do the job?"

I frowned. I was tired of playing around.

"And what is this job I may be leading them to?"

84

"It's a safety deposit box in a Merchant Bank in the city. I want you to get what's inside."

"I presume this box contains stolen goods."

He laughed and the coughing started again. When he recovered he mimicked my prissy tones.

"Stolen goods! Too right sonny. Lighten up. Don't be so uptight. You work for Albie so don't come the innocent with me. Stolen goods! That's a good one."

He laughed and wheezed again.

"I can't believe Albie didn't tell you all this."

I kept silent. He touched my arm.

"There's absolutely no risk to you. I've got all the documentation here and the key. You'll have all the documentation from me. It's simple. I've had years to work it all out."

He looked at me closely.

"You are just right for the job. Albie chose you well. Not only do you look the part, you are the part. A tight arsed little brief who looks like butter wouldn't melt in his mouth. Perfect."

"I wanted a respectable solicitor with no previous and you are the spit for it. It'll be over in no time. Albie said you were a good brief with no whiff of anything dodgy so the bank'll let you take it without a quibble. Albie will get his cut and so will you. And if you pull it off the slice will be a big one."

He took a bulky envelope from his breast pocket.

"It's all here – the documents, my authorisation and the key."

He paused.

"Well, are you up for it?"

I pretended to hesitate. One of my first lessons was never to seem too eager when you are dealing with old cons. He grasped my wrist.

85

"This is the easiest money you'll ever make lad. Even with the percentage to the fence, and Albie has plenty of tame ones in his pocket, we're looking to clear at least three million. You and Albie stand to get a quarter for a few minutes' work. He drives a hard bargain that bastard."

I took the package and checked it. It was all there. My passport to the vault. He held up the key to the safety deposit box and a deep velvet bag.

"Put the lot in there. I'll stay in the taxi outside. Then we'll go back to my gaff."

He patted my arm. I pulled away. I don't like to be touched.

He grinned and did it again.

It worked. Back in his hotel room, he emptied the bag on the bed. On the dark duvet, the stones shimmered, caught in a shaft of light through a gap in the closed curtains. Diamonds do nothing for me but I can see why some people get addicted. He was one of them and he gently touched the pile and moved the stones around as they glittered in the light. I watched his expression. It was like getting a fix or savouring a prolonged orgasm. He closed his eyes and caressed the stones.

"They're perfect," he breathed.

I opened the whisky bottle I'd got on my way back. It was a strong malt. I poured him a glass. He gulped it and I gave him another. He fingered the diamonds again.

"These are what kept me going all the years inside."

He took the bottle and reached for a second glass. I shook my head.

"Not for me. I don't drink spirits."

"You really are little Master Perfect. You're the only sodding brief I've known south of Watford who doesn't drink like a fish. Still you handled it well. No complaints."

I clicked on my mobile phone.

"Just letting Albie know we've done it."

"No."

"He took the phone from me and clicked it off."

"Let's sit back and talk. I've been having a good think about things while you were in the bank."

"He sprawled in the chair and peered up at me over the rim of his glass.

"You do realise that Albie has not been entirely frank with you," he began slowly.

"Well he never told me about the diamonds or the deposit box if that's what you mean."

He waved his hand dismissively.

"No, not that. Haven't you asked yourself why he picked you for the job?"

"You said so yourself. You wanted a brief with no previous."

He shook his head,

"No. Albie has plenty of tame of tame older briefs he could choose from. Why pick you? A rosy arsed sprog. Mind you, I'm not carping. You did a good clean job but it could have turned out tricky. I'd have thought about having someone with more experience if I'd been Albie. He is always very careful. That's why they have never managed to put him away."

He drank again and I noticed his speech was becoming slightly slurred. After his years inside, the strong malt was having an effect. He brushed aside drops of sweat beginning to form on his forehead. He pointed to the pile of diamonds and ran his fingers through them again. The sunlight had gone and they now looked like a pile of dirty melting ice.

"Suppose I suggested that we split these two ways. Just between the two of us. No cut for Albie."

He saw my expression as I stiffened.

"Now wait. Think about it. You won't get an opportunity like this again for a long time."

"Albie's done a lot for me. He's been like a father to me."

"But he's not your father."

His voice was harsh and he was now sweating heavily.

"He's not your father," he repeated.

I was angry.

"My real father left us when I was a little kid, He's dead. He was a shit. I never knew him."

"Did your mother tell you he was a shit?"

I shook my head angrily.

"If it hadn't been for Albie—"

He reached out and gripped my arm.

"That's why I'm offering you half of this."

"I don't understand."

He took a deep breath.

"The name on the documents I gave you. It wasn't my real name."

He didn't bother to pour another glass but drank straight from the bottle. He began to cough again and gasped for air. He slumped in the chair, his eyes fixed on mine."

"My real name is Bernie Flaxton."

I stepped back. I shook my head. I didn't want to know.

"It's true," he said, his words now becoming more slurred. "I didn't leave your mother. It was Albie. He wanted her, always had since we were kids. Always wanted what I had. I'd always got the women he fancied since our school days. He was jealous of me. He fixed it

88

so that I got caught after the job when I stole those stones. He was the one who killed the Hatton garden dealer not me. I was set up from the start. The filth didn't catch up with me for a few days after the robbery so I had time to arrange the deposit box. He knew I'd stashed them somewhere but didn't know where. He couldn't do anything till I was out. I guess your mother was too frightened of him to ever tell you the truth. Probably kept quiet to protect you. It must have amused the bastard to send my own lad to collect the stones. Just the sort of thing that sick bastard would do, He's a psycho you know. Always was. I bet he gets a real hard on knowing you're here with me. Did he tell you to get rid of me once you'd got the stones?"

He sat up and looked at me closely.

"He did didn't he? I was to have an accident once you had got them."

He coughed again and this time the spasm was worse. He struggled for breath. He pointed to the diamonds which sparkled as another shaft of sunlight came through the curtain. He reached out and pushed them towards me.

"Here take the lot if you like. I owe it to you."

He closed his eyes as the spasm suddenly got worse. He clutched his throat and struggled for breath. He began to choke.

I knelt beside him and put my arms round his shoulders and held him tight as he began to shake. There was nothing I could do. The nerve agent I had put into the whisky bottle was now acting quickly. I held him until he was still.

I knelt there for a while and thought about the situation. Then I eased back into the chair and gently closed the eyes of the man who said he was my father. Did I believe him? There was always something a little too pat about the story of my father abandoning us and recently I had begun to wonder. The last time I had seen my mother at the hospice I think she had been trying to tell me something about my father. I'd wondered at the time but done nothing. She had begun to talk about when I was a baby but at that moment Albie had entered the room and she had stopped when he had put his hand on my arm and promised to take care of me. I think she was frightened for me as the old man had said. It could be true. It all made sense. I knew Albie always got a perverted thrill when I described in detail the hits he sent me on.

Until now his open sadistic pleasure at my description of the kills had amused me. It made me feel superior to him. I had prided myself on being ice cold, dispassionate, a professional. The targets were just objects to be eliminated. It was just business for me. This time the buzz for him would be overwhelming. I wonder if he would have told me what I had done, that I was just a pawn in his twisted game. Another to be manipulated. I think he would. I doubt if he could resist the perverted pleasure it would have given him. It was true. Albie was a psycho. It was never just business with him.

I looked down at the corpse. The face was peaceful. I felt no emotion as I wiped the spittle from the side of his mouth. I had never known him. He was a stranger and his death meant nothing to me. Even if what he said was true, I wasn't going to get screwed up by that old Oedipus guilt. Guilt was for losers. But I thought of the years my mother had been forced to keep silent and put up with Albie for my sake. The anger welled up inside me as I realised the life she had really had and for a moment I had difficulty breathing. I stood and gradually regained control.

I checked the whisky bottle. There was half left. More than enough for Albie.

About the author

Don Nixon is a writer living in Shropshire. He has had a number of short stories and poems published in magazines and anthologies in the UK and North America. In 2004 he won the Writers' and Artists' Yearbook short story competition and this encouraged him to write. He has won various competitions for short fiction and poetry and for the past two years has won the formal poetry category at the International Poetry Festival at Lake Orta in Italy of which Carol Ann Duffy is the patron. He won awards at the Deddington Festival and at the Liverpool Festival last year. This year he won the Leeds Peace Poetry Prize, gained a short story award at the Steyning Literature Festival and had a short story published by the HG Wells Society. He has had two short stories published by Bridge House in the *Scream* and *Going Places* anthologies. Poems were published later this year by Chester University Academic Press and Descant Magazine, Toronto. A film company has shown an interest in a crime short story – *Santa's Grotto* – he wrote for Tindal Street Press in the anthology *Birmingham Noir*. Later this year his novel in the Western genre – *Ransom* – will be published.

The Weapon

L. A. Wilson, Jr.

Riley Jacks watched as the car barrelled through the red light like *a bat out of hell*.

Through his tranquilizer-induced calm, his eyes struggled to keep up with its motion. It side-swiped a parked car, jumped the curb and headed straight for Myron Edelman; the man he'd been following.

Edelman just stood there frozen, his mouth wide open as the car bore down on him. The car's rear end clipped a fire hydrant sending it into a spin. The passenger-side slammed into a young woman and knocked her seven or eight feet through the air before she landed face down on the pavement. Its nose crunched into a street lamp and climbed up a foot or two right in Edelman's face. A man who looked to be in his mid-twenties jumped out of the car in a dead run and disappeared into the traffic and the crowd.

It was happening so fast Jacks' mind couldn't keep up with it. The guy had tried to run Edelman down. Jacks thought about shooting him, but he wasn't sure Edelman was worth it, and by the time he made up his mind the driver was gone.

Edelman was shaking in his shoes. He stood there staring at the woman's body before backing away. Jacks started across the street after him but Edelman was walking away, slowly at first, then briskly.

Jacks crossed the street. He would have to run to catch Edelman now.

But it was the woman who caught his eye. She was lying on her stomach with blood smeared across her face. Jacks looked back toward Edelman; he was merging with the crowd, getting away. The tranquilizer held Jacks still, made him think. He practiced being a callus son-of-a-bitch, but this was way too much, even for him. He pulled his attention away from Edelman and knelt beside the woman. She was alive. She groaned and rolled to her side as he touched her shoulder.

"Hey. You all right?" he asked.

But she didn't answer.

Her eyes rolled across their sockets, open but perhaps unseeing. She might have been pretty at another time, but there was a hard edge to her looks. She had a large raw abrasion on her forehead where the pavement had chewed up her skin.

"Hey, lady!"

He leaned forward and grasped her shoulders. He didn't see her move, but he heard the click.

"Get away from me!" she hissed followed by a string of obscenities. There was a pistol in her hand – a pea-shooter, a two shot derringer anchored to her wrist with a spring-clip.

The soft wail of sirens crept into his ears.

"Get away from me," she warned again as she dragged herself backwards.

His eyes locked onto hers. He had seen enough killing to know when somebody was serious about it. The sirens were getting louder.

"I'll kill you, you *sonuvabitch*! I'll kill you!"

She dragged herself to her feet and staggered away through the crowd of astonished onlookers.

Jacks looked around. Edelman was gone. The driver was gone. Nothing was going right for him. The sirens were almost there. He faded into the crowd too. He wanted another dose of medicine, but his pillbox was empty.

He looked for a bar as he left the scene.
Any kind of medicine would do.

Myron Edelman liked black women, not that there was anything wrong with that. He even married one. The problem was, according to his wife, she wasn't the *only* black woman he liked, so he kept on cohabitating with one after another until he gave his wife the gift of syphilis for Christmas. That was more of a mistake than any man needed to make during one lifetime.

So Angela Edelman wanted to be rid of Myron, that's what she told Jacks. Get rid of him and everything that reminded her of him, except for his money. Jacks had no problem with that, because she was willing to pay whatever it took to accumulate enough details of Myron's infidelities to give her and her lawyer a walk in the park.

Myron hadn't been difficult to find again. All Jacks had to do was to station himself in a poor Atlanta neighbourhood and wait for him to surface once more.

According to Angela Edelman, her husband fancied himself to be a record promoter. He had made some money back in the seventies pushing Motown wannabees. He probably would have had more success if he hadn't spent more time seducing his talent than developing it. Now he was searching for the next great rap star, but his appetites kept getting in his way.

Jacks huddled down in an alley next to a dumpster where he could watch the activities in the building across the street. He pulled his coat up around his neck to ward off the early October chill.

Edelman was visible through the disrupted blinds. There was a woman with him, but Jacks couldn't see her clearly. They were talking. Edelman was reaching toward

94

her, and then he moved beyond Jacks' field of vision.

He heard the sound of approaching footsteps and pulled his coat higher. People usually gave a wide berth to men loitering in alleys.

"Get the hell out of here!" A harsh and belligerent voice assaulted him.

Jacks grunted and pretended to be drunk.

"Didn't you hear me?" the voice came again. "Get your goddamned homeless ass outta here! Don't make me have to tell you again, goddammit!"

Jacks turned his head enough to see who had approached him. He recognised the face although his only previous encounter with it had been brief. It was the driver – the man who had crashed his car trying to run over Edelman.

The man was startled when Jacks straightened up. He had apparently not expected anyone who might challenge him. There was a muscle-bound hard-ass with him, so Jacks took his hand out of his pocket.

"You know what this is?" Jacks conspicuously dropped a small metal object...

The man looked at him curiously.

"Here, take a look at it."

Jacks stepped closer to the two men.

"What do you want to do – shoot me, cut me? If I drop this grenade, you'll be dead before you even think about running."

"Hell, I ain't in this," the second man said.

Jacks pulled his pistol with his other hand, and the driver stood there frozen.

"If I shoot you, nothing happens, but if anything happens to me, we all die."

Jacks smiled at him. He liked screwing with tough guys. It gave him a certain satisfaction and a sense of power that the pills stole from him.

The driver snatched a pistol from his belt and called Jacks' bluff.

"Then we all die," he said.

"I'm gone," the second man said. "I'm gone." He started backing away. "I didn't sign on for this."

"Shut up!" the driver yelled.

"What are you doing here?" Jacks said.

"You first," the driver replied in a voice much calmer than the situation demanded.

They stared at each other, then for a fraction of a second the driver glanced away. Jacks followed his line of vision. He was scrutinising the same apartment Jacks had been watching, but the light had gone out.

"I'm gonna walk away," the driver said. "You do what you gotta do."

Jacks let him go. There was no good way for crap like this to end. He felt the second man's pain. This was deeper than the job he had signed on to do. He slid the fake hand grenade back into his coat pocket. He needed more answers, more money, or both.

"You got your nerve coming over here and getting in my face over something like this."

Angela Edelman was posturing. Her neck was working overtime. Jacks suspected she did a lot of that. It was part of her personality. It made her appear in control.

"What good is he going to do me dead?" she continued. "I want his sorry ass healthy so he can cut me a cheque."

"Who do you think would want him dead?" Jacks asked.

"You mean bad enough to hire somebody to kill

him? Hmmph. Why don't you ask some of his street whores?"

"Street whores don't pay for killings. If need be, they do it themselves. These were gun-carrying locals. They don't cost much, but they ain't amateurs."

She slumped into a chair and sighed. "I don't wish Myron anything bad. I'm over him. I simply don't care anymore."

She stared out of her bay window overlooking Niskey Lake. Jacks recognised a kind of sadness in her. Myron had kept her well. She lived on Atlanta's south side hidden among the famous who themselves lived anonymously amongst the nouveau riche. It was a life she had no desire to leave, and without Edelman, had no ability to maintain. Killing Edelman was certainly not in her best interest.

"I'll pay you extra to make sure Myron stays alive," she whispered.

"What?"

"You heard me." She didn't look at him.

"How much?" He felt bad about asking that question, and her scowl almost made him regret it.

"Two thousand dollars if you get me what I want."

"No problem."

What she wanted consisted of names, times and pictures. She wanted to know if Myron was low enough to jump any of those fifteen-year-old-rap-wannabees. She wanted to slap him so hard he'd negotiate anything just to keep it out of court. Jacks just wanted enough money to dump his antidepressants. Cash could be a wonderful mood elevator.

It's hard to remain anonymous in the city, especially for a person who revels in his reputation.

97

They call it *going for bad*. Somebody had to know "the driver" and Jacks knew how to drag the streets for information.

The driver's name was Ramar Tate, a man known for doing almost anything but nothing particularly honourable. He wasn't a professional killer, just someone who was willing to kill – if the price was right. Suddenly he had become an important part of Jacks' life. Myron Edelman needed to stay alive so that Angela could get paid, and Angela needed to get paid so that Jacks could get paid.

Jacks watched Tate make his customary rounds – the brief stops, collections and intimidations that provided him sustenance at the expense of another's weakness. A man like that needed killing, just for the hell of it.

Def Watch Records was a curious stop.

Jacks followed him inside and scowled with a practiced expression that dared the receptionist to ask him anything as he walked past. Carriage and attitude meant everything if a man had the nerve to use them.

This was Def Watch's uptown office, away from the hood – a location calculated to prevent the millions of attitude-waving brothers and neck-popping sisters from realising that their frenzied support kept Jake Stein laughing all the way to the bank.

"You move, *mothafucka*, and I'll waste your ass!" The owner of the unexpected voice put a muzzle in Jacks' back and confiscated his guns.

"Damn!"

Jacks had that sinking feeling like a ton of very bad crap was about to fall on him. His little ploy hadn't worked. The receptionist must have called one of Tate's boys from out front as soon as he had walked past her.

"Don't kill him in here!" Stein protested after Tate's

man had forced Jacks into his office. "Get him outta here. I don't want this shit connected to me."

"You're Riley Jacks, ain't you – that crazy ex-cop?" Tate asked as he perused his quarry. "You still carrying that fake hand grenade?" He grinned maliciously. "What the hell do you want anyway?"

Jacks shrugged. "Why are you trying to kill Myron Edelman?" he said.

"Who?"

Jacks tried not to show his surprise. Tate's response had been genuine. He was sure of it, but he had to push harder.

"What about it, Jake? You the man around here. None of the rest of these boys got enough juice to pay for a killing."

"You're in way over your head, Jacks, and it's gonna cost you," Stein growled.

"Edelman's worth money to me, Jake. Whatever your problem is with him, let's work it out."

"Where you're goin', you ain't gonna need no money," Tate sneered.

Tate stepped closer to Jacks. He jammed the pistol's muzzle against his head.

"You're showing up at too many places where I happen to be," he said. "I don't know what you know, but you won't know it for long."

"I said, get him outta here," Stein repeated. "I won't have this in here."

Tate hustled Jacks down the back stairs and into an alley in spite of his protestations and attempts to explain. He was without weapons and outnumbered, and they didn't give a damn about his spying for Edelman's wife. He was simply a problem that they didn't need to have. His purpose wasn't even relevant to them. They whacked him on the head and shoved him into the trunk of a car. He could feel it moving. It stopped briefly, and then accelerated again. He suspected that they were on the street now. It was stop and go – transient stops followed by rapid acceleration. At the next stop Jacks popped the trunk and hit the pavement running.

Stupidity was a common thread among the criminal element. It was hard to find a new car without a child-proof trunk anymore. The blare of horns and the screech of brakes followed him as he dodged cars in the afternoon traffic. The bright sun accentuated the throbbing in his head and almost made him blind. Even so, he could see Tate and his accomplice bearing down on him. He made it to the sidewalk and stumbled through crowds of pedestrians. His eyes desperately scanned his surroundings. There was never a policeman around when somebody really needed one.

His eyes settled on a bank. He ran as fast as he could, but they were gaining on him. He made it to the glass doors and tried to decelerate to a nonchalant walk. He smiled at the security guard, a man in his early sixties with greying hair.

"Excuse me, Sir," he greeted the guard cordially.

The guard returned a pleasant smile and started to respond. Jacks stepped on his foot, grabbed his arm, twisted him around and had his gun before the old man could blink.

"Sorry," he said before stepping back through the glass door and planting two bullets in the chest of Tate's partner who had the misfortune of being the closest.

Tate froze and started to back away as onlookers screamed and scattered.

"You can't run that fast, man," Jacks warned. "You're not after Myron Edelman?" he asked.

100

"I got who I wanted. I just didn't finish the job yet."

The barely audible sound of police sirens sang in the distance.

"I don't think either of us wants to be here when this goes down," Tate said.

Jacks never ignored wisdom regardless of the source. He lowered the weapon and backed away, and they both disappeared in opposite directions.

Jacks felt like he was on the run. He didn't relish having killed one of Jake Stein's men, but the way things were going, he'd probably have to kill some more before he could find a way out of this. Killing was always a bad thing, but a person could get away with killing a thug or someone too poor to matter. Anyone could do it once, but multiple kills incited too much attention. That made the police obligated to look harder even if they didn't really care.

Jacks slouched in a rear corner booth at *The Castle*. It was a place without windows, a popular way of building clubs thirty years ago when black lights and Day-Glo posters were all the rage. He chewed on a burger that tasted like it was cooked in last week's grease. This wasn't a place where Jake Stein would look. They still played B.B. King and Bobby "Blue" Bland rather than the hip-hop rhythms that garnered Jake his money.

Wrong again. Jacks realised that when he stepped into the street again. A young white guy in a black business suit leaned against a Mercedes with tinted windows parked in front of the club. He came to attention as Jacks exited the building. White people didn't come here unless they were bad-asses. Bad-asses could go anywhere. Race was no impediment to real bad-asses.

Jacks started up the street to his left and the man

shifted to intercept him. Jacks changed directions, and the man shifted again. He sized the younger man up. He was too old to outrun him, and he didn't need to kill anybody else today.

"Mr Jacks! I'm not here to cause you a problem. I've been instructed to give you something," the young man said.

Jacks surveyed the empty street before easing the pistol from his belt.

"Who's in the car?"

"A benefactor," the young man said.

"Get him out of the car."

"I'm afraid I can't do that, Mr Jacks. Our benefactor prefers to remain anonymous."

"Look…"

"Mr Jacks, why don't you take a look at what we're offering?"

The man reached gingerly into his inside pocket using two fingers and retrieved a fat envelope. He dropped it on the pavement between them on Jacks' instruction. Jacks counted ten one-hundred dollar bills and lowered his weapon to a less threatening position.

"Who do I have to kill for this?"

"Our benefactor wants you to keep that as a down payment."

"On what?"

"On seeing that things turn out right," the young man explained. "We've been told that you are a man who can arrange for things to turn out right."

"What things? What the hell are you talking about?"

"You're the detective, aren't you, Mr Jacks. You'll figure it out."

The young man opened the driver's door of the Mercedes.

"Our benefactor wants you to know that Jake Stein has no interest in Myron Edelman," he said before starting the engine.

"What? What do you mean? How does he know that?" The Mercedes moved away leaving Jacks without an answer. Suddenly everybody wanted to give him money. Maybe his luck was finally changing. He just didn't know what he had to do to keep it that way.

The one place that Myron Edelman didn't seduce women was at his home. That's why he was never there. Edelman knew his wife was having him followed, and his home was such an obvious point of surveillance that he simply never used it for anything except sleep. Jacks had long ago stopped wasting his time watching Edelman's condominium, but not on this night.

Edelman almost jumped out of his skin when Jacks appeared at his door. It was a secured, high-rise condo with absolutely no access without a security card. Only two kinds of people could broach that kind of security – very *big* people or very small ones. Jacks knew the small people – those who serviced the well-to-do. A janitor was willing to look the other way to repay a favour.

Edelman threatened to call bodyguards. He threatened to call the police.

"I'm not here to hurt you, Myron. All I want is a drink and a chat."

Edelman just stood there with one of those trapped expressions on his face.

"Your wife is really pissed with you, Myron. You screwed up big-time."

Something about the casual tone of Jacks' voice must have relaxed Edelman because he seemed to relent and stood aside to allow him to enter.

"Yeah," Edelman sighed. "Tell me about it. You've been following me. You work for her?" He poured Jacks a rum and coke without asking his preference.

"Yeah, she wants your money, Myron. I guess I do too since she's paying me."

"I see," Edelman said. "You the one who tried to run me down or has she hired more than one of you?"

"Not me, Myron. I want you to stay healthy. I worried about Angela for a minute, but I don't think so. If you die, it gets to be a *helluva* hassle getting paid. Angela wants to lay up in that luxury house overlooking Niskey Lake. She doesn't want any part of a murder case."

Edelman looked perplexed.

"You've been in the wrong place at the wrong time twice."

"Twice?"

"You don't know about the second time, but don't worry about it. Still, it's too much of a coincidence for me. What about you? What do you know about Jake Stein?"

The music business was cut-throat, and the rap scene seemed saturated with people who didn't have a problem with violence. Edelman, however, was such a minor player that it was unfathomable that he could be a serious threat to any of Jake Stein's interests.

Suddenly Edelman's eyes got big. He started to stand. His mouth opened, but no sound escaped.

Jacks didn't move. He had seen the shadow from the corner of his eye and knew someone was behind him.

"I'm not your enemy," Jacks said looking towards the figure bent over in the shadows. "And I won't be unless you do something stupid."

Slowly Jacks turned and faced the pea-shooter for the second time.

"I could take both hits from that and still beat you to death." Jacks smiled when he said it, but his voice was deadly serious.

"Please, Beverly. Don't do this. I'm all right."

Edelman moved quickly and encircled her with his arms. There was a gentle sincerity in his actions as he led the woman to the couch and cushioned her head with a soft pillow.

"She thinks she has to protect me." He laughed a soft self-deprecating chuckle.

"No she doesn't," Jacks replied.

The woman stared at Jacks. The look was belligerent and defiant, but there was something else there. Jacks recognised it from a lifetime of reading people. She was carrying a truckload of pain, and being in love with an aging married man couldn't have been all that deep.

"What's your name?" Jacks asked. "Beverly who?"

Edelman answered for her. It seemed his protective nature was working overtime.

"I'm not the womanizer Angela thinks I am, not that it should matter to you. I do, however, have obligations."

Beverly Jones was seventeen when Myron Edelman discovered her, so he said. She was going to be the next Diana Ross except for the fact that she was just a bit short on talent. When Edelman concluded that her career was not to be, he consoled her in his usual way, but ultimately that wasn't enough either. It was hard for a young girl to get what she needed from a married man's leftovers. Eventually she drifted from Myron to drugs, then to prostitution. For what it was worth, it seemed to have hurt Myron deeply, because he really had developed a genuine emotional bond with her.

So after a lot of wasted years, he sat there on the couch pouring out his guts to the man his wife had paid to stick it to him, and it was beginning to dawn on Jacks that even Myron might not have known the real deal.

"What's between you and Stein, Myron?"

Edelman's eyes quickly flashed toward the woman, but he didn't answer.

"Look, your ass is in trouble. People are following you, and they aren't your friends. Stein's people are after me because I stuck my nose in this, and I had to pop one of 'em today. You ain't a fighting man, Myron. You need all the help you can get before somebody kills you."

"He's not the one they want to kill," the woman replied.

Jacks stared at the abrasion on her forehead. Everybody had been trying to tell him, but maybe his tranquilizers kept him from listening.

"They want me, but it's too late. I'm already dead."

Her voice was husky and as hard as what was left of her beauty.

Edelman patted her shoulders and rubbed her back in a consoling manner, although it appeared that she didn't need it. The pain in Edelman's eyes told Jacks that he was actually consoling himself.

Beverly had fallen victim to the big disease with the little name. Her words. She was dying and talked as if she was reconciled with her fate. It was something that Jacks had seen before and all too frequently. She was a woman who had made bad choices but had arrived at the understanding that, at best, she had to live with them, and at worse, die with them. Although it was Edelman touching her, her eyes remained fixed on Jacks. People like that recognised their contemporaries. He was as empty as she was. She had just filled her emptiness with a deadlier placebo. He felt the pressure of his pill box in his pocket, but it didn't comfort him.

"I want you to take me somewhere, Riley Jacks," she announced.

Edelman reached for his hat.

"Not you, Myron, just Jacks."

"What... why?" Edelman began.

"There's something I need to do, and I need Jacks to help me do it. Besides, Mr Jacks' burning curiosity is killing him. He wants to know if all of this b.s. swirling around him is likely to interfere with his money. A favour for a favour, Riley Jacks. You help me and maybe I'll tell you a story."

"I can help," Edelman protested.

"No you can't."

The finality in her voice ended the conversation.

"I think Jacks and I understand each other. You understand what you want to understand, Myron. It's not your fault, and I don't dislike you for it."

She hugged him for a long time – long enough to make Jacks feel like an intruder. He turned his back and walked toward the door.

Beverly only told Jacks where she wanted to go after she got in his car.

They rode in silence for a while before Jacks decided how to talk to her about what she was doing.

"I don't think this is a good idea," he finally said.

"No need to worry. Jake Stein's a wimp. He won't do his own killing, besides, you'll be there to watch my back and make sure things turn out right." She managed a smile that touched him in spite of himself.

"Hell, what's this about, lady? Why can't he wait to see you dead?"

She sighed and lit a cigarette. It made her cough, but

she smoked it anyway.

"I couldn't afford the medicine," she began. "It was ten or twelve grand a year. I took it on and off. Most of the time I didn't take it. I had met Stein through Myron back when I was singing. He could see that I was sick, and I was desperate. He said he would pay for my medicine if I would do this one thing for him."

She paused for a long time, and stared out of the side window as if she had no intention of continuing.

"What?" Jacks said.

"Sometimes..." her voice choked, "sometimes you do bad things because you have to." She turned back toward Jacks with tear-dampened cheeks. "Jake Stein didn't own Def Watch. He just acted like he did. His father-in-law owned the business. I guess Jake got tired of watching the money pass through his hands without stopping, so he asked me..." her voice faded briefly, "he asked me if I would be available at a birthday party for his father-in-law."

Jacks listened with unrestrained curiosity. He listened to what she said, but more importantly, he listened to what she didn't say.

"Available? Available for what?"

"What the hell do you think?"

"Wait. Wait. He knew what was wrong with you, right?"

"That's why he wanted me. Jake Stein wanted to be rid of his father-in-law. Tate could have shot him, stabbed him or run him down, but it would have all pointed back to Stein. What could you say, though, about a grown man stupid enough to catch AIDS from a hooker? I was his sixtieth birthday present. Don't look so shocked. I still looked pretty good with make-up and without these cuts on my face. Anyway, he paid for the drugs for about a

108

year then I guess he decided that I wasn't dying fast enough. He didn't like having someone alive who could testify about what he'd done."

Jacks brought the car to a stop across from the entrance to Stein's office.

"What's the plan?" he said.

"Myron won't leave me alone. He's got the guilts. No reason though. I was a big girl. One of these days we'll make a wrong move and Ramar Tate will kill him too, just for the hell of it. I don't think I could bear that. I'm going to beg Stein to leave us alone, convince him that I won't talk. I won't live another year anyway."

She got out of the car, and Jacks started to follow, but she stopped him. She needed somebody to watch her back, to make sure that Ramar Tate didn't sneak into the building before she was finished.

Jacks waited in the car. He had a bad feeling about this, but it wasn't his play. He didn't know what he was doing there. Maybe he was just seeing that things turned out right.

Several minutes passed, and the unexpected blare of approaching sirens split the air. An ambulance and police cars blocked the street as frightened people ran from the building. He listened to Stein's employees repeat the story as they led Beverly from the building in handcuffs. She had walked in as cool as a cucumber, popped him twice in the head with that pea-shooter, then sat down and smoked a cigarette while they called the police.

With Jake Stein dead and his father-in-law sick with AIDS, the value of Def Watch dropped like a rock. Before it was over, Myron Edelman acquired the company for a song, and Angela Edelman got paid without having to go to court. The way she and Myron grinned at each other, it wouldn't have been surprising if they ended up bed-mates before the check had cleared. Money cures a lot of pain.

Riley Jacks emerged from his bank having deposited the four-figure cheque he received from Angela Edelman. A familiar young man exiting a black Mercedes approached him.

"I have the balance of your payment, Mr Jacks, and our benefactor would like to speak to you." He handed Jacks an envelope and directed him to the Mercedes.

The tinted rear window opened slowly revealing an attractive middle-aged woman dressed in black. She wore dark glasses, and her fingers were drenched in diamonds.

"I wanted to personally thank you for seeing that things turned out right, Mr Jacks, she said in an elegant and subdued voice.

Jacks accepted her handshake but remained at a loss for words.

"I... uh... I don't know what you think I did, but..."

"You saw that things turned out right, Mr Jacks, whether you intended to or not. My father thinks he was just unlucky. He doesn't know what my husband did to him, but at least I have some satisfaction in knowing that evil will not triumph."

The tinted window slowly rose to end their conversation, and the Mercedes pulled away. This wasn't difficult to figure out. Jacks just couldn't understand why Jake Stein didn't. A man can't kill his wife's father and expect to continue business as usual.

Another two-thousand dollars. He perused the newspaper while he waited for the next teller. The local news was boring except for the arrest of a suspect in the recent murder of an unidentified man in front of the Union Bank. An anonymous tip led police to the murder weapon, which had been stolen from the bank's security guard and was found under the seat of a car belonging to a street criminal named Ramar Tate. Jacks grinned broadly. Jake Stein's wife had been prophetic. Things did have a way of turning out right after all.

About the author

L. A. Wilson, Jr. was born in Norfolk, VA and grew up on the coastal plains of North Carolina. He is a graduate of North Carolina Central University and Meharry Medical College and currently lives in Atlanta, GA with his wife and children. He is a member of The Mystery Writers of America and his works have appeared in Alfred Hitchcock's Mystery Magazine, Night Terrors, The Edge and Detective Mystery Stories.

Nominated for the 2012 Shamus Award for short fiction by The Private Eye Writers of America for a publication in the Jan/Feb 2011 issue of Alfred Hitchcock's Mystery Magazine.

Stevie's Luck

Gerry McCullough

Okay if I sit here, mate?

Ta.

Nice quiet place this, I like it. Fuller than usual to-night, or I wouldn't butt in like this, see?

Buy you a round?

Och, no problem, lager is it?

Bit quieter than the dive I was in a few weeks ago. Fights breaking out all the time, there, so they tell me. There was a bad row even the once I was there, I'm telling you.

Bad.

I missed out on the worst of it, I'm glad to say.

Let me tell you about it. Don't mind, do you?

Don't usually go to this *Drummond* place, like I say it's a bit of a dive, never know what might be happening, bad stuff, maybe. It was Marie wanted to go, my usual's the *King's Head*, a bit more upmarket, but Marie says the Happy Hour in the Drummond's real good value, so, hey, I goes along with it.

Place is jumpin' when we gets there, Thursday night, wouldn't expect it, but maybe news about this Happy Hour stuff's got around. They've done it up since I was last there, lotta red paint, hanging baskets, coupla tables outside – like, who's going to sit there more than a coupla days a year in our climate? Oh, right, it's for the smokers, isn't it? You see them outside all the pubs now, shivering and smoking away, must think it's worth it. I'll smoke outside on a fine night, but not the sorta weather some of them put up with. The flowers in the hanging baskets inside are a bit droopy, from not getting watered much, I'd bet. You need to look after flowers, water them enough and not too much. Nobody gets it right. That's the sort of thing I care about. I'm sensitive, me.

I used to look after the flowers and plants when I was a kid. Mum never bothered, or she'd drown them and they'd be dead in a day or two. I told her not to bother after a while. I took care of them.

Mum wasn't that good at any practical stuff, come to that. She was a lovely woman, not very tall, slim, delicate sorta girl. I've got some snaps of her here, you wanta see? Lovely, right? Coulda gone on the films, I used to think. She and me got on fine, especially when I was a kid. She was a popular lady, always some fella or other chasing after her, but none of them mattered to her like I did, or that's how it seemed to me, right? Sometimes one or other of them'd move in for a while. I didn't mind, long as he didn't cause me no pain. She kept them in line, made sure they behaved. One guy, I'll never forget him, he was called Jimmy, he lifted his hand to me one day when I'd been giving him a bit of cheek, called him a baldy ould git, as I remember it. Well, Mum was down on him like a ton of bricks, and he was outa the house, bag and baggage, the same afternoon. That's what she was like.

Money? Well, I don't know, she managed okay, never seemed to be short, don't really know where it came from. The dole, I reckon, and maybe my da sent her some from time to time. It wouldn't have been anything else, see, if that's what you're suggesting!

She changed a bit as I got older. Stopped being so protective. But there weren't so many of the men after her by that time. She was getting a bit rough looking, tell you the truth, by the time I was sixteen or so. Musta been all the drinking. Lines on her face. Hair needing touched up, and she often didn't bother, so the grey was starting to show every now and then. Couldn't seem to talk to her any more, way we used to. She'd get angry, right out of the blue, sometimes, and turn on me. She was the only one I could trust, from when I was a kid, and then I couldn't trust her either. I moved out a year or two after that. Hey, sad story, right?

My da? I dunno where he was. Don't even remember what he looks like. Only what Mum used to say. Only saw him two or three times, when I was the size of sixpence.

Mum said we were well rid of him.

Okay, so here we are in the Drummond, Marie and me.

Marie's looking all about, seems to be expecting someone. She's dressed up real nice, short narrow skirt, lots of eyeliner, fluffy blonde hair pulled up on top of her head and a few curls hanging down on her smooth neck that's all brown from the sun, and this sharp, spicy perfume. Top so low cut you could see gleams of white flesh where the suntan ended. Maybe she'd like me to tell her it makes me fancy her, but, hey, it's not good for chicks to think they've got you going. Gives them a big head, makes them think they can push you about.

I wasn't looking bad myself, mind. I'm not all that tall, but so what. I look a bit like Sinatra, the chicks tell me, before he got old and wrinkly, in the first pictures he made, you see them sometimes on the late night movies, or you get them on DVD, slim figure, thin bony face, smooth good looks. When all the chicks were howling for him, right? Not saying they're all howling for me, but I get my share okay, see?

Mum used to say I looked the image of my da.

Before she went into the home, that was. When she could say anything that made sense.

She came round to see me one day, maybe ten years

ago now, and started ranting and raving and threatening me. Seemed to think I was my da. Didn't recognise me. Didn't talk any sense. End of it was, I had to call the doctor, and they said she needed to go into an institution, for her own safety. Not to mention mine, the look in her eye when she started shouting at me and lifting the kitchen knife and coming at me, well, I had to get out quick, I'm telling you. Nothing else for it.

Senile dementia, they called it.

But she wasn't that old.

I always remember her the way she used to be, when I was a kid, when she made a fuss of me and told me how handsome I was, just like my da. Showed me a photo of him once, but when I asked to see it again, she'd burnt it, she said. When I try to picture it, all I get is Frank Sinatra in his younger days. But I reckon that should be close enough.

I like to dress right for the look, dark coloured shirt with the turned down collar and a real smooth light coloured tie, blue to show up my eyes, see?

So, when Marie started looking all round, I says to her, "Hey, what's up, babe?" Not that I was really that worried, but you gotta make an effort, make them think you're interested, it's half the battle.

"Nothing," she says. She gives me a look, and I squeeze her bare knee under the table, and I can see I've got her going, right? Then she says, "See Porky anywhere?"

I don't. Don't want to.

"How would I know where Porky is?" I says.

"Thought you were talking to him on the phone the other day?"

"Hey, that wasn't Porky," I said. I laughed. "You've got Porky on the brain, kid! Waiting for your next fix,

115

right! You mustn'ta heard me right. That was my bookie!"

"Oh, right," she says. "Just, I was hoping to see him. I've got the cash for some gear," she couldn't help telling me, though she knows I don't like that sort of stuff.

I'm getting sick of sitting there without a glass in front of me.

"Buy me a drink," I says.

She's still looking all ways, like, but she heads off up to the bar

That's what chicks are for, right?

Totally.

Porky, I have to tell you, is a guy I can do without.

Full of shit, okay? In both senses.

See me, I'm not into all that stuff.

The odd bit of blow, yeah, but the gear, like, that's another whole bag of trouble. Not for me.

What Marie does is her own funeral. Totally.

Hey, that wasn't a bad sort of joke, right?

He does other stuff, Porky, beats people up to order, I'm told, but that's not something I would have anything to do with, either, right? Gotta look after yourself, keep clear of all that stuff. I look after myself, always have done, nobody else's going to do it.

So I'm waiting for Marie to get back over with my drink, when this fella comes up to me.

"Stevie McCartney?" he says.

I give him a look.

"You owe me big time," he says.

I know who he is. Joe Murphy, from the bookie's.

Big red faced guy, with a crooked nose. Used to do some boxing.

So I know he's been waiting to collect from me for the past month, on account of I missed out on last month's payment, but what I don't know is how he knew to look for me in the Drummond, which is like a dump I never go to, and I was starting to wonder about Marie, but, hey, she wouldn't squeal on me, not Marie.

She comes back then with the booze and I can see they know each other.

"Joe."

"Marie Bas. Hi, babe. Good to see ya."

It makes me wonder again.

I grabs the drink, and, what about it, it's lager.

So I bangs it back down on the table, so's a big gollup of it spills. Makes a bright goldy sort of pool on the tabletop.

"I don't drink that muck, Marie," I says, keeping my voice calm. "You know that rightly. Bacardi. Tequila. Either. Even a good vodka. Not lager."

What's that, mate? Oh, right, yeah, a tequila'd be great. Ta.

Good stuff, that. Thanks. Feel like I need something tonight, don't know why. Just need a bit of comfort, sort of.

Right, so, where was I?

Marie was looking upset.

"Stevie, maybe just this once – it's a promo offer, see? Quid a pint."

I just gives her a look.

"Stevie I've only got the money for Porky, and I need it bad. Till the giro comes in. You know. I gotta have the stuff regular. I can't…" She trails off and tries smiling at me.

Joe, the ignorant git, interrupts.

"Talking about money, Stevie Wonder," he says with a big ugly grin on his chops.

"All right, all right," I says. "You'll get your money. End of the month. Swear it."

Joe grabs me by the front of my shirt, drags me up on my feet, bangs my legs against the edge of the table, not that he cares less. He's some size, the boyo.

"Know what, rat face? Not the end of the month. Now. Or it'll be too bad for you. I'll have to tell big Shamie you've been a naughty boy, see?"

If you think Joe's a big one, you oughta see big Shamie. My teeth's starting to chatter and my legs is wobbling and I feel sorta sick.

There's people all around, lined along the bar, crowded into booths, standing about with their glasses in their hands. And nobody paying no heed. They turn away, look into their drinks, talk all the louder, laughing about nothing. I could be dead in a second or two for all they care.

Marie grabs Joe by the arm.

"Let him go, you big bully, you! He hasn't got no money! You can't hurt him! You said—"

"Hasn't got no money, you're telling me? Then," says Joe, leering at her, "I just wouldn't like to tell *you* what's gonna happen to him, babe. Not the kinda stuff to say to a lady like you, see."

Marie bursts into tears. Then she starts scrabbling in her handbag.

I can't see too well what she's doing, with the way Joe has my shirt scrunched up round my neck so's I can't hardly breathe, but I can sorta see, out of the corner of my eye, right, that she's taking something out of her bag, a white envelope, maybe.

"Here!" she says, and she pushes it at him. "There's that fifty quid in there. You know. All I got. Leave Stevie be. Give him a chance to get the rest of it together, okay?"

"Chicken feed! His bill's in thousands!" says Joe. Then he looks at her and he musta changed his mind.

Fancies her a bit, maybe.

"Okay, babe," Joe says. "End of the week, right? Not any longer!"

And he drops me back into my seat, looking sorta contemptuous, like, and brushes off his hands. As if he wants to get rid of the feel of me. "Don't know what you see in this dirty wee squirt, Marie. A right lump of scum," he says. "You can do a lot better for yourself." And he walks away.

So then Marie throws her arms round me and she's all huggin' me, like, till I has to say, "Whoa, whoa, girl! Everybody's looking."

They were, too. Voyeurism, it's called. Anything sexy, they're avid, especially one fat git staring down Marie's top. But, hey, if someone looks like getting beaten up, that's another story, right? Time to look away. And I'm wondering about the stuff going on between Marie and Joe Murphy. How would she think he should know she has fifty quid? And what's with the "You can't hurt him! You said..." bit? And I was starting to wonder if Joe gave her the fifty quid to tell him where he'd find me.

Still and all, she's done a really nice thing, hasn't she, giving Joe her drug money to help me, so I says, "How's about getting outa here, babe?" and I takes her hand and move her outside, round the back alley, and I let her kiss me.

The half moon was out by then, and a star or two twinkling in the dark navy-blue sky, and there was just a sweet warm summer breeze touching our cheeks and lifting Marie's hair enough to make it look like, what's that stuff, gossamer, and the smell of the creamy honey-suckle and the pink roses in the hanging baskets, and Marie's own scent, sort of spicy and oriental, and it was really getting to me.

119

And, I'm telling you, I couldn't help feeling a bit of a stir when I looks down at her with her arms tight round me and putting everything she has into the kiss, and half her acid green top dragged off with the action, like, and I thinks, "Hey, guess what, maybe I could do worse?"

Never reckoned on a live-in girl friend, and still don't want one, but maybe Marie and me could see a bit more of each other? I knew she'd been wanting to. Things she'd said. Maybe it was time I rethought our relationship? I hadn't thought she cared all that much about me, compared to the drugs, hadn't thought I could trust her, well, you can't trust anyone, can you, specially druggies on H? But maybe I'd got her wrong?

And, hey, if she'd been up to something with Big Joe, sure, she didn't want anybody but me, now, did she?

Then she opens her eyes and looks right up at me, her mouth still fastened on mine. She's smallish, right, Marie, and her body just fits good against me, and I could feel her all the way down pressing close against me, and I have to tell you, honest, I felt my legs go all trembling.

It was, like, something special, see?

Hey, what's this, another tequila? Hey, it's my round, mate. Well, okay then, if that's the way you really want it. Cheers, mate!

Any road, we goes on snogging for a bit, and then I goes, "Okay, babe, let's do it!" But funny, she pulls back and says, "Hey, wait a minute, Stevie, I gotta go to the bogs," so I acts cool, though I'm, like, ready enough. I steps back and I says, "Don't be long, babes," and I gets out a fag and lights up while she skips off.

And that's where I might feel a bit guilty if I wanted to, right, because if I hadn't let her go back in there, it would have been different.

But, hey, what else could I do?

I stood there and leant against the white washed stone wall and smoked, and I wondered again about Joe Murphy. And about Marie and Porky.

So the fag's about done, but I'm not, like, get me? And there's no sign of her coming back. I'm starting to wonder what's keeping her, when I hears this racket going on inside.

I goes over to the back door of the pub, with its new bright red paint, and I open it a bit, thinking, like, it'll be a gas to see what sorta fight's going on.

It's not that easy to see, what with all the guys crowding round, but there's Marie, right in the middle of it.

I open the door a bit further, but I make sure to keep well behind it. Out of sight, like.

I can see big Porky. I nearly yelled out at him, but I got myself stopped in time.

He's a huge guy, hard to miss.

Hard fat, they call it. Muscles as well as bulk, see? And his ginger hair shaved to nothing.

I never liked him.

Ex para military, heavy into the drug scene these days. Not the only one, like. Trouble, for sure. A man to keep away from. But Marie hasn't the sense to do that.

What, you going, mate? Oh, just heading up to the bar, right? Yeah, I'll stick with the tequila, ta.

Where was I? Yeah, Porky's useful in a sort of way, see? Useful to Marie, I mean. Any road, he has the drug franchise, like, for round here.

Doesn't bother me. I don't need him. I keep clear. Like I told you, I don't go for the hard stuff.

He's standing there with his hands on his hips like some ould targe of a woman, his face stuck out forward with a glare in his eyes I wouldn't want aimed at me, and he's yelling at Marie.

121

And give it to her, the girl, she's yelling right back at him. Up close and personal, as they say.

"You owe me!" Porky yells.

"Only one bag!" Marie yells. "Peanuts!"

"Can't do business that way," Porky grunts. "Pay on the nail, that's how it goes. If you want some now, you pay up front, right!"

"So I don't have the cash, okay?" yells Marie back at him. "Whatta you want from me, tell me that? Blood?"

Funny her saying that.

I knew rightly she's spent her last, paying Joe off for me, and it sorta crosses my mind I should maybe give Porky the twenty-five she owes him? Maybe I should help her out this time? But sure, what difference would it make? She could manage without it for once, right? Do her good! She shouldn't be so hooked on the stuff!

Anyway, I don't want to talk to Big Porky at all. I'd rather just have nothing to do with him.

I've my hand in my pocket, fidgeting about with the roll I won on the scratch card Wednesday, coupla hundred, but I've got plans for that. Horse called *Stevie's Luck*, couldn't lose, a name like that. Mind, I wasn't far off giving it to Joe earlier on, when he was near choking me. Would have if Marie hadn't jumped in.

I'm trying to make up my mind, when the real trouble starts.

Tommy Moore and three or four of his heavies comes into the pub.

You know Tommy, right?

Got out on the Good Friday agreement, and kept away from the political stuff. Went for the drug dealing instead.

A wee shrimp of a man himself, with the wedgie heels on his cowboy boots to give him more of a height. Not just small enough to be in a circus. But the boys with him

122

makes up for it okay.

Another round? Thanks, mate! Like, I'm real chuffed to get talking to you tonight, mate. I sorta felt like I needed someone to talk to. A good listener, right? Anybody ever tell you you're a good listener, mate? Make a person feel like you're really interested, see? Hey, I must be getting a bit bluitered here, listen to me getting all sentimental.

So, Tommy Moore and his heavies come into the bar, right?

He was looking for Porky, I heard after. Porky'd been muscling in on Tommy's territory, it seems. Not happy enough with his own patch, the big eejit. Tommy and the boys were here to teach him a lesson.

Well, that's what they do, everybody knows that. If Porky'd been cheating on Tommy, he was asking for it.

"Hey, Porky!" Tommy goes, all friendly like. "Glad to see you sticking to the Drummond, boyo!"

"Yeah, right, this is my patch, Tommy, you know that," says Porky. You could tell he was dying with nerves, but doing his best not to show it. A huge big fella like Porky, and Tommy hardly up to his chin, but Porky was shaking in his trainers. It was kinda funny to see. I couldn't help laughing.

Tommy's lip was dripping with sweat, and he had a funny grin on his thin wrinkled face with the red cheeks and the droopy pouches at his jaw line. He was a lot older, I could see, than he'd like people to know. Oughta get a facelift, like Joan Collins.

"So it's a funny thing, Porky," Tommy says softly, "but somebody was telling me they saw you dealing blow down the King's Head Monday night, Porky. That's a funny thing, isn't it, Porky? And an even funnier thing, I'm told you were dealing the gear on the Tuesday night, Porky?"

123

Every time Tommy says 'Porky', his voice seems to go up a bit higher and get a bit louder. He's moving up closer to Porky all the time, and Porky's sorta trying to slide back a bit, without being too obvious about it. Marie's moved back a step or two, I'm glad to see, and I was wishing she'd get herself on over to me at the back door and out of it, but I suppose, like the rest of us, she was too hooked on watching what was going on. A right soap opera, so it was.

"No, Tommy, you've got it all wrong," Porky starts stammering out, he's turned a weird sorta colour, like a dirty white, like his mammy doesn't use Persil.

"Wrong, am I, Porky?"

Tommy sounds ever so soft and gentle.

For about half a minute.

Then suddenly he's screaming.

"Get him, boys! Take him out the back!"

Then there's a lot of action that I mostly don't see too well, what with everybody crowding round, and what with Tommy mentioning the back door, which made me pull my head back, thinking I'd be as well getting away from there myself. I just caught sight of Charlie, the Drummond bouncer, out of the corner of my eye, and he was dodging away out of the picture, making for his post at the front door, there's just one of him, see? And then, like, I think I hear Marie doing a bit of shouting.

Seems Porky's pushing her in front of him, trying to keep away from Tommy and the boys.

There's punches being hurled all directions, and a lot of screeching and stuff, and I stick my head round the door again, and I'm just wishing I could see better when there's a gleam of metal and one of the boys is pulling a knife.

So then I'm pretty pleased to be so far back and out of

it, and I look round to make sure no one's coming up behind me and I can get away okay if I want to.

It's fine, a clear exit, good enough.

I takes another look round the door, just interested to see what's going to happen next, like, and then for the first time I gets a good view of Marie.

Porky has her by the arms in front of him, with her back up against his fat belly, like one of these human shields you hear about on the news, and she's, like, struggling to get free and not getting any joy out of it, and I starts wondering to myself if maybe I can do something for her, but, hey, what could I do with all these big guys?

It all happened in a minute.

I can still hear Tommy shouting, "Get him, boys!" sounding just like a big baby yelling for sweeties, and everybody else is screaming and bawling away, and Marie's looking round, sorta wild, with her fair hair coming down over her face and her green top dragged lower than ever. Then I don't rightly know but I've a sorta idea she sees me, peering round the door, and her face changes and goes all soft, like she thinks I'm going to come riding in on a white horse and rescue her, but, hey, my shining armour's away this month for a polish, and just as she seems to be catching my eye the fella with the knife kinda makes a lunge at big Porky, and Porky sorta swivels round and drags Marie further in front of him and the knife goes thrusting up right into her belly.

I see her face going white and her eyes dreadful and a big gollup of blood, like, spurting out of her, and then I'm outa there.

Down the back alley and on the first bus back to my own flat, right?

And the door locked and no lights showing the rest of the night.

She died in the hospital, not long after they got her admitted, I heard.

Nobody knew I was ever there at all. Except Joe Murphy, okay, but he was long gone and not wanting mixed up in it, so, far's I know, he never said nothing, right?

They were looking for witnesses, but, sure, I couldn't have told them much any road. All I saw, like, lotsa people saw more. Up to them to spill their guts if they weren't worried about what Tommy Moore might do to them later.

I kept my head down and no one came near me for a bit.

Sure, I'd missed mosta the excitement with being out the back all along, hadn't I?

One of Tommy's guys got arrested, they tell me, but there wasn't anything on Tommy, well, naturally. He hadn't even been armed, and no one was saying anything much that would tie him in with it.

And nobody knew Marie had anything to do with me. Well, she hadn't, by then.

And, hey, it was her own choice to go there, nothing to do with me, all I did was go along with her. None of it was my fault, not in the way I see it.

See, I'm not a criminal. Never did anything all that bad.

Never had anything to do with big Porky, and less still with that Tommy Moore, so my name never got mentioned.

I was right out of it.

Lucky, wasn't it?

Yeah. Totally.

126

Like, I've had a lot of luck, see? Mind you, the flippin' horse came in sixth. Still, you can't always be lucky, can you?

But, hey, I was lucky meeting you tonight, like. Dunno why, but I felt like I needed someone to talk to. That's not me, not usually, right? Know who I am and what I'm doing, don't need anybody else propping me up, not me. Got my life organised the way I want it. See, I'll tell you a secret. You don't want to let anyone else get too close. Not so's you start caring too much about what happens to them. Start that, and you find yourself getting right and messed up. Look out for yourself, make sure things go your way, that's the thing. I've been doing that since I was a wee kid, and I'm telling you, it works for me.

Why're you gettin' up? What, chucking out time, is it? Give me a tick, I'm trying to get up, here. What was it I just said, don't need anybody to support me, like? Got that wrong, didn't I? All those tequilas, mate!

Going my way?

Well, maybe you might give me a hand. Looks like it'll have to be a taxi for me, this time. What was it you said your name was? Bas?

Hey, just like Marie? Nothing to her, are you?

What did you say? It means 'death' in the Irish? Funny, that.

You want to turn off down this alley?

Right, mate, whatever you like. It's a shortcut, a bit dodgy, right, but hey, there's two of us, okay? You'll not be needing that knife you've got there, mate, but does no harm to have it ready, yeah?

It must be my eyes, mate, that last Tequila, maybe? But you're looking sorta funny all of a sudden.

Got a lot taller or something.

And your face, it's gone sorta bony.

127

Hey, like you're getting more like a walking skeleton sorta thing every time I look at you now! And, like, with wings, or somethin'? Like a picture I saw yonks ago, the Angel of Death, is that it?

Funny. Must be my eyes.

Listen, mate, you're my friend, right?

It's really good I met up with you tonight. Lucky, that's what.

But see me, I'm always lucky.

About the author

Gerry McCullough, born and brought up in North Belfast, graduated from Queen's University with a BA Honours in English Literature and Philosophy, and an MA in English Literature. She has been writing since childhood, with more than fifty short stories published, some of them prize winners; her story *Primroses* won the Cuirt International Award. Her regular podcast of her own Irish stories has proved immensely popular, with listeners in the thousands. In November 2010 her first full length novel, *Belfast Girls*, was published by Night Publishing and has proved to be a considerable bestseller. This was followed by *Danger Danger* in 2011, and a collection of short stories, *The Seanachie: Tales of Old Seamus* in January 2012. The first book in her Angel Murphy series about a feisty Belfast girl, Angeline Murphy, *Angel in Flight: An Angel Murphy Thriller*, was published in June 2012, and will be followed shortly by the second in the series, *Angel in Belfast*.

Foxtrot

Don Nixon

It's not easy nowadays to find a man who can do a good foxtrot.

Most of the ones who picked it up under the twirling silver globes of their local palais in the 50s and 60s are now dead, stuck in a care home or jealously guarded by possessive wives.

I've always loved the foxtrot.

That delicious pause as you check your step and then release into the glide. Even now it can give me goose bumps. Fred, my late husband, used to say it was like making love, though being brought up strict Chapel, I never liked to encourage him in that sort of talk.

That Thursday afternoon I was on my own at the seniors' tea dance the Housing Association puts on every week for the retired people in the Tower Block. I always look forward to Thursdays and the tea dance and it helps me to keep fit. I was listening to Glen Miller's 'In the Mood' but had nobody to dance with. Myra my usual partner had a hospital appointment for her veins and I was doing my best to avoid old Bill Shuttleworth of the clammy wandering hands and peppermint breath.

It was then that I saw him.

Our secretary had mentioned she was bringing a visitor and that it was an unattached man who could dance. That had caused quite a stir among those of us who were used to dancing bust to bust and having to negotiate who was going to lead. Indeed arguments over who was to take the

129

lead had soured many a friendship between some of us widows. Rachel Holroyd and I don't speak any more after the fiasco of the Age Concern tango competition but one of these days I'll get my own back. I'm a good hater. The prospect therefore of this new man who could actually dance was an exciting prospect. There was an expectant buzz in the room as the secretary introduced him. He stood in the doorway. It was strange to see him again after so many years.

The hair was probably dyed and the stomach was suspiciously flat, probably held in by a support but there was no doubt in my mind that it was Leo Kemp. Many nights when I was having my breakdown, I had fantasised about ways to inflict a painful punishment on him should we ever meet again. I've never told Myra about the compulsion I had to wash my hands after my feverish imaginings of getting my revenge on Leo. No doubt she'd start quoting *Lady Macbeth* at me. Myra is the intellectual one in our group and got a certificate in English Literature at the Tech last year. She persuaded me to go with her to see the play before her exam and it was after that the hand washing started again. I can never see why Lady Macbeth is made out to be a villain. After all she was a good wife and loved and supported her husband.

Leo Kemp!

The fraudster, the thief, the seducer of gullible women and the man who was certainly responsible for the death of my husband over twenty years ago. What fools Fred and I had been to be so easily taken in. And it had been mainly my fault. Fred had always done what I told him.

He glanced around the room. I thought of a fox taking his time before he pounced on a henhouse full of plump chickens. His eyes slid past me. I took a deep breath to steady my nerves. I'd recognised him but he hadn't recognised me. Years back when we'd met in the Tower Ballroom in Blackpool, I'd been a bottle blonde but with Fred long gone, I'd let it grow out and for years it's been a wispy white that I cut myself. I suppose really I've let myself go though I keep fit with the gym class. I certainly was a far cry now from the fifty-year-old he'd danced with in the Tower Ballroom in Blackpool when he'd launched that scam that was to cost poor Fred his life. But I still like nice things. He clocked my Gucci bag and Harvey Nicholls dress. Since I'd come up on the lottery I've really taken to spoiling myself.

He crossed the floor. He moved well. If they did a senior citizen version of *Strictly Come Dancing* on the Telly he'd be a shoo-in. I noticed the jealous looks I got from some of the old biddies clustered round the Tombola table and got a sudden stab of satisfaction.

They say vanity is the last thing to go.

"May I have the pleasure?"

I rose to my feet and immediately we moved in strict tempo to the middle of the floor. He could certainly dance. After the uncertain tugging and pulling of Myra, this was heaven. He was a slightly built man and after bulky Myra I had to resist the urge to lead but I soon settled into the rhythm. For a moment I forgot all about the past and let myself drift in his arms as he guided me through a sequence of steps that seemed effortless. I felt myself physically responding to him. I hadn't been this close to a man since Fred died. I sniffed a heavy cologne. The same as the one Fred used to wear. His one extravagance. The thought of my husband dragged me back to reality. This was the chance for the revenge I'd been waiting for all these long years. I forced a smile.

"You're new here."

He nodded.

"Yes. Just passing through. Haven't been up north for years. Some business. I met your club secretary at the Masons last night and he told me about your retired club's tea dances and invited me. Said they could always use an extra male."

I managed another smile.

"That's certainly true. It's the problem with being retired. We are mainly widows here. Most of us have to dance with each other. It's not the same."

"I bet it isn't. Especially for an attractive lady like you."

He grinned. The dentures were certainly not on the National Health.

I glanced up.

"We can always use a man here," I said slowly.

"Good. Glad I came then. I like being used."

He smirked at the innuendo in his tone and pulled me towards him. We did a series of perfect turns.

"Do you live here?"

"For the last few years. It's a housing association. All of us here are retired. I have a flat on the top floor. It's got a marvellous view."

I found I was relaxing and my tone was quite normal. Nobody would have guessed I wanted to kill him.

"Are you local then?"

"No," I lied. I didn't want him to associate me with the town of twenty odd years ago. There was always the chance something might jog his memory and he'd get suspicious. I quickly improvised.

"No. I'm from Manchester originally. I came here after my husband died to live with my sister. She's gone now so I live here alone."

"You're a widow then. That must have been hard."

I baited my hook.

"Well my husband left me very comfortably off and it's years now since he passed away. And I believe in enjoying myself"

"You do right," he said. "You can't take it with you."

I wondered if the secretary had told him about my win on the Lottery.

"And just how do you enjoy yourself?"

The innuendo was blatant.

"Well last Christmas I went on a cruise to the Caribbean."

"Phew! That must have set you back a bit."

"Who cares?" I trilled. "It's only money."

"Did you go with a friend?"

The question was a little too casual.

"Oh no! I haven't got anyone that close and I think you need to be comfortable with someone to go on a cruise with."

I looked up at him.

"Mind you it would have been nice to have someone to dance with."

He pulled me a little closer.

"I do so agree. The last cruise I went on I was on my own and was quite lonely."

I nodded sympathetically and felt the pressure of his hand on my back. I leaned against it. Two could play at this game.

The pace was slowing and the brass was now muted. The saxophone gave an orgasmic moan. In the old days it had been the signal to get closer. He bent down to whisper in my ear.

"I imagine you get a terrific view of the Pennines from

the top of this building. Didn't you say your flat was at the top?"

I nodded.

"They were telling me last night about Pendle Hill at the hotel. Isn't that one of the tourist sites?"

I pointed to the large picture window that ran on one side of the hall. The great whaleback of Pendle stood out clearly on the other side of the valley.

"That's Pendle," I said. "There's a lot of tourist twaddle about it and the Lancashire witches but the witches did actually live around there."

"I find history fascinating," he said.

He sounded really interested. It was incredible the way he could so easily adapt to what you were saying. I think that's how he managed to get through to Fred who was nobody's fool when it came to money except for that one and lethal time.

"I'd love you to show me the place. When I'm travelling on business I like to see the local historical sites and you're clearly an expert. Did they actually kill anybody?"

I was on safe ground. I go to the Tech. Historical Society and they had just done some lectures on the Lancashire Witches.

"Nobody knows for sure. Most of them were demented old crones like Mother Demdyke and her brood but one of the coven is very difficult to fathom. Her name was Alice Nutter and she was a gentlewoman. Lived in a manor house by Pendle. Nobody has ever come up with a plausible explanation of why she was mixed up with the witches. I don't suppose she thought killing was such a big deal. Probably enjoyed the excitement. Catching the victim unawares. Gave her a buzz as they say. I did a psychology course at the Tech last year. They call that sort of thing compulsive behaviour."

I thought of my hand washing and Lady Macbeth. I smiled to myself and wondered if Alice Nutter had ever killed a man out of revenge. Perhaps I could make my fantasy real. I made up my mind. I knew just what to do.

Another record began. This was my chance. I fanned my face and pretended a tiredness I didn't feel. "I think I've had enough of dancing today," I said tentatively. "If you're interested in Pendle and the witches, come up with me to my flat if you like. You get a good view from my window and I've got a pamphlet about the witches the local historical society produced.

As a matter of fact I had a good win on the Lottery some time ago and gave the Society the money to print it."

His eyes gleamed.

"I'd love to. It's a bit noisy in here to talk. And you are such an interesting lady. I'd like to hear more. It's fascinating."

He gave what he thought was a sexy smile. He really was full of himself. I smiled back. He was hooked. I moved to the door.

"I'm afraid the lift's out of order," I said casually. "We'll have to use the stairs. It's seven flights up."

He set off at a brisk pace which soon slowed. The stairs run round a well and at the sixth floor he paused and leaned against the guard railing which stood between us and the void. He straightened up and tried to control his gasping. I do the stairs every day and was hardly out of breath.

"Only another flight," I said encouragingly. I wanted to hurry. At any moment someone might come out on to one of the landings and see us.

Finally we were at the top landing. He leaned against the low rail. In spite of his attempts to control his breathing, he wheezed and slumped forward his chest against the railing, his arms hanging loosely over the barrier, his head down. He looked exhausted. For a moment I was alarmed. Was he going to cheat me? A heart attack wasn't punishment enough, not for what he had done to Fred.

It was on this landing that Fred had finally given way to despair. The scam that Leo had cunningly concocted had left my husband penniless and in debt. Fred, unable to face me had climbed these stairs and at the very place where his tormentor now stood gasping, he had climbed over the railing and jumped.

I slipped quickly behind my foxtrot man. I put my lips close to his ear.

"I think you knew my husband years ago," I hissed. "Look down there. He's waiting for you."

I grabbed hold of him at the back of the knees. Anger gave me strength and I was fit. Most of his weight was forward and his upper body was slumped over the rail as he fought for breath. He was too feeble from the climb to struggle and I'm strong and wiry. I lifted and for a moment he was stuck horizontally on the top of the rail, his arms flailing as he tried to reach back. The railing buckled.

"Remember what you did to Fred Greenhalgh, you bastard," I screamed.

I pushed hard and gradually he slid forward. He tried to shout but the climb had left him breathless and only laboured grunts came out.

I watched him as he fell. He seemed to fall so slowly, arms spread-eagled like those pictures you see of sky divers on the television. I was surprised how little noise the body made as it smashed into the concrete at the bottom of the stairwell.

At that moment I felt I could understand Alice Nutter. Killing was no big deal. I went to wash my hands.

About the author

Don Nixon is a writer living in Shropshire. He has had a number of short stories and poems published in magazines and anthologies in the UK and North America. In 2004 he won the Writers' and Artists' Yearbook short story competition and this encouraged him to write. He has won various competitions for short fiction and poetry and for the past two years has won the formal poetry category at the International Poetry Festival at Lake Orta in Italy of which Carol Ann Duffy is the patron. He won awards at the Deddington Festival and at the Liverpool Festival last year. This year he won the Leeds Peace Poetry Prize, gained a short story award at the Steyning Literature Festival and had a short story published by the HG Wells Society. He has had two short stories published by Bridge House in the *Scream* and *Going Places* anthologies. Poems were published later this year by Chester University Academic Press and Descant Magazine, Toronto. A film company has shown an interest in a crime short story – *Santa's Grotto* – he wrote for Tindal Street Press in the anthology *Birmingham Noir*. Later this year his novel in the Western genre – *Ransom* – will be published.

The Most Whimsical Jape of the Season

Kate Tough

The fact is, we were all friends of Carol's. Gus had been the price you paid.

Somewhat selfishly, Carol had died in a slapstick mishap involving a high wind and a giant 'D' (it's still unclear what she was doing in that part of town) and since then, Gus has regularly invited us all for dinner – ostensibly to show that he is doing OK, "Absolutely fine, yes, yes, absolutely."

He certainly seems his usual self.

I'm sure everyone in this room has had the same thought – give it another month and I can refuse his invitations without looking like an unsympathetic bastard.

Real reason for the dinner parties?

Gus knows the window of pity won't last forever and he has one chance to make her friends his friends. And before you go thinking, isn't that exactly what I'm doing? Let me say no, it is not. The difference between Gus and me is that he actually wants these people for his friends. I'm only here to point-score against Helen, in that post break-up, *They're my friends too* way. The, *Why should I give up our friends because you've decided it's over and dumped me?* routine.

A transparent charade? Maybe.

I wanted to piss her off – wanted a reason to get in touch even if it was for an argument. Specifically to start an argument. Had to get back in her head and hang around for the afternoon, *You may think you've finished with me, lady, but I'll decide when you've finished with me.* The usual stuff.

Arse! To think I fought for the prize of sitting round

the table with this lot. Tears were spilled so I could be here and not Helen. In the normal run of events it would have been a Pyrrhic victory. A triumph until half-an-hour after arriving, when I'd have realised that Helen knew fine well I had nothing in common with 'her people' and that I'd be hating every minute. That I had not a single real friend in the room and to demand to come was pathetic. Perhaps this would have upset me to the point where I'd have wondered if I had any friends of my own to spend the evening with. A crack in the veneer. Fuck. Then *she'd* have won this round.

As it turns out, though, I WIN! I WIN! because I'm in mortal danger and she won't find out till it's too late, thereby ensuring she is forever wracked with survivor's guilt. I've no problem admitting how happy that makes me. A result in anyone's book.

Everyone who was invited this evening turned up; no-one's babysitter cancelled, no-one 'came down with something'. So if, as Gus announced twenty minutes ago, none of us is leaving here alive, there won't be anyone to strike it rich on the chat show circuit; "I was supposed to be there but the twins had a rash. Decided to stay home with the Merlot I'd bought for Gus. He was a bit of an authority so you had to choose carefully. And now here I am... *sniiifff*... Alive... *sniiifff*... and feeling deeply, deeply *guilty*."

Wankers.

It's too much to hope Gus is going to burst back in carping, "Had you going there, didn't I? Eh? Eh?" in his excruciating office-joker mien. If he did, I'd congratulate him on the premium jump in his usual humour. He is the opposite of consummate, whatever that is – after he left the dining room and locked the door, he made his rehearsed speech about our imminent deaths while craning his head through the double-door serving hatch in the wall. 'Uncool' doesn't go nearly far enough. Usually you can respect an unhinged killer for his cultivated aura of passionless detachment. Being kept hostage by this enthusiastic boy-scout is just embarrassing.

But maybe I'm a sick bastard too because I'd rather turn up at a dinner party and be murdered by a psycho than turn up at a dinner party and hear the same old conversation about how much school fees are affecting house prices, or whatever it is they whine about. Bunch of Michael Bublé fans. Spent so much time worrying about paedophiles they took their eyes off the sociopath ball and now look what's happened. If you choose to spend your life fretting, you should be happy when something goes horribly wrong. Vindication is a good feeling, no? Ingrates.

Incidentally, on which birthday do you wake up knowing that now it's time to wear a sweater on a Saturday night? I'd expect it if I was in my fifties. I'd rather not be around it in my thirties. Thirty-nine is still thirties.

I know, I know, I begged for a seat at this table. I'm being too hard on them perhaps, but I am under a small measure of pressure right now. If we'd got to the after-dinner drinks this would be easier. Poor show, Gus, you flipped before the brandy was poured. I need a bloody brandy.

No. They're not bad folk. The common denominator in this room is merely a lack of imagination. Which is, I hate to admit, where Gus has one up. While they've been on the internet pricing decking, he's been thinking pretty damn far outside the box. Bless him.

Couples, who were holding tight to hands and forearms, are starting to ease back into their chairs. So far, not much is being said beyond the, "What's he playing at?" vein. "Maybe he's watching from a camera behind the mirror," "Maybe there's a microphone hidden in the hostess trolley." You can tell which women are the daytime TV watchers. 70s sleuth to the rescue.

We're not about to make any sudden moves because on exiting the room, Gus left his dogs behind. During dinner they were two daft Staffies. Now they are bull terriers. Heavy-set, skulking thugs that finish what they start. Brushing about our feet we hear their wet, nasal breathing. At some point they could get restless. I am making friendly clicking sounds with my tongue when they pass, reaching my hand kind of near them, as if to pat. These overtures will put me at the bottom of their list.

The smell of used dinner-plates and room temperature leftovers is too much. I'm out of my chair, knocking on the hatch. "Gus! I don't know what you're up to, but enough's enough. Open up. Two single nougats and a ninety-nine." No reply from the little double-doors. A murmur in the room about not upsetting him. Yeh, whatever. "Gus! Open up! If this is one of those murder-mystery dinner parties, you should have asked first. Games are shit, Gus. None of us wants to play because none of us wanted to be here anyway. We only came 'cause we felt sorry for you. Now we *hate* you. OPEN THE DOOOOR!"

Nothing.

As I sit back down (four dog eyes following me) footsteps clip across the kitchen and the hatch flies open. "Right, right, sorry for the delay everybody, I just had to, eh, get the room ready. Multi-socket adaptor fused but it's sorted now, so we're good to go… and no shouting. Did I hear someone shouting? OK, ahem… RIGHT! Hands up who likes me! Come on, show of hands, who likes Gus? Who is Gus's friend?"

There are more dirty looks directed at me than at him just now. He's misjudged the level of terror. The delay in

141

proceedings has taken us down from a seven to a four. So if he was expecting wholesale compliance, that's not the mood of the room. Parent-teachers' meeting is more the vibe.

"Gus, I'd like an explanation of what exactly you think you're doing," says Head Parent. "You cannot hold us in a locked room."

"I need to use the bathroom," says Nice Wife, with a hint of apology for the inconvenience. I'll admit I'm slightly relieved he didn't hear my outburst. I give it to him again, kind of. "Joke over, Gus. Very funny but it's time to open the door."

"What about the game of poker you promised us?" says a v-neck.

You'll find in life that it's not until a critical moment that you learn about the pointless waste of friendships of convenience. It comes over you in a tawdry wave of shame and regret and you can't express the horrible realisation precisely because you don't know the people you're with well enough to communicate at that level. I'd rather be dealing with this alone right now, than be alone in the midst of this shower.

And being all nicey-nice to Gus recently, because it was easier than telling him we wished he was Carol, has backfired in a big way. Firstly, it meant we came to his house tonight and secondly, we have no negotiating power. We didn't like him enough to get to know him and now we don't know how to appeal to his better nature; don't know how to work him.

I try reasoning with him, "Put your own hand up, Gus. Put it up your arse and then come through here and let us out." I stand, with thoughts of approaching the hatch and strangling some sense into him. And then I sit down. There's something unsettling in the way he is appraising us. Perhaps we do need to deal with this collectively.

"I have a gun." He holds up a pistol. "Amazing what you can buy on the internet. You should see what else I've got set up in the morning room. Anyway, this" – he waves it about – "is the reason you are going to put your hands up if you like me. Sheila, if you really need the bathroom, use the trifle bowl." The chairman of our parent-teacher meeting requests clarification, "Do you want us to put our hands up now, or do we wait for Sheila to spend a penny?"

"Now dammit! Put them up NOW!" When he shouts, the dogs pace and growl and hands fly up – all except mine. There's a clammy sheen on Gus's face, like he's taken a little something to help him through with this malarkey. Not really Gus's style, drugs. Maybe it was an extra thrown in with the gun deal. He's got a look about him like he's observing himself, trying to work out what he's doing while he's doing it. I sink a bit inside. If the person you are dealing with is under the influence, you're lost. You can't reason with an altered state. I've never understood people who argue for hours with a drunk.

"Lying bastards," he says. "Look at you all with your arms in the air. *Please sir...* I know fine well you can't stand me. This was your chance to come clean. Ohhhh. At least Carol was always straight with me. She married me so she didn't need to work. You people are so polite it's cruel." He points the gun through the serving hatch, holding it steady with both hands.

"Not voting, Monty?"

"Nope."

"Quite right. I like a man with the backbone to be honest. We could be friends, you and me."

"Nope."

"Of course we could. You tell it like it is, same as I do."

143

"You tell it like a floundering headmaster. You... are a twat."

Somebody whispers for me to shoosh and stop winding him up. I want to vomit at the way they're scared of him.

"Who else thinks I'm a twat?" Gus asks.

The hands are faltering, coming half way down and going back up and creeping back down, stopping half way. Nice one, Gus! To lie, or not to lie, that is the excruciating question. Everyone's looking to see where everyone else's hands are.

"Pathetic," he spits. "You're still at it. You don't know whether to tell the truth or tell me what I want to hear. Inbred arrivistes. I'm going to enjoy the next bit very much." The hatch closes. I conclude my fellow guests are facing imminent death.

A crew-neck whispers, "What are we going to do? We have to get out! We have to jump him."

"What about the dogs?" asks Head Girl. Good point.

"Have any of you ladies got Valium?" I ask. "This is not the time for modesty. We won't think any less of you. If you have some, whip it out."

John opens his wallet to extract a sheet of pills. "Not the man I thought you were, Johnny boy. Never mind, give it here."

I press two pills, what the hell, three pills into a square of cheddar. I drop it under the table and when the first mutt picks it up I drop another other chunk for mutt two. He scoffs it.

"OK. As long as Gus waits five minutes before he comes in, it should be safe to overpower him."

Five seconds are all we get. The key turns and Gus and gun appear. He is making a Barbara Woodhouse gesture with his hand: posture and vocals all stiff and ridiculous.

What a tosser. But an excellent dog-trainer of a tosser, it has to be said. His alert command, "Danger, boys, danger," has them growling and prowling. Any movement in the room not sanctioned by Gus and they'll explode forward. Consequently, it's no great feat for Gus to get a single file of acquiescent diners through the door. I am told to stay put. He leaves a dog behind to make sure I comply.

Fido is watching from a respectful distance. Because my body can't move, my mind works overtime. Never again will I say 'yes' to an invitation I'd rather say 'no' to. I think about Helen. The way I've obsessed for days over how she ended the relationship, how she spoiled our happiness; it's her doing, it was *her*, it was *her*. In this captive moment something tells me it was my doing. It was *me*.

The dog slumps to the floor and I'm up out my seat. I check the windows but they're locked. Placing a chair under the serving hatch, I step on it and feed myself through head first. I have to move the toaster and kettle along the counter to give my body somewhere to be while my feet catch up. Contorted between the work surface and the wall cupboards I nearly laugh but find I'm not in the mood. By rolling my body slightly my feet drop to the floor. I pull the hatch closed in case the dog wakes up. Gus's planning has been remarkably accomplished thus far, so I'm not surprised when the back door, the kitchen window and the kitchen door are all locked. If there is a phone in here I can't say, hand on heart, I'll use it. Of course it's sad, the snuffing out of innocent lives. But not as sad as the snuffing out of important lives. Or my life. Jesus, what is that? Is that a hairdryer? What the fuck damage can he inflict with a hairdryer? That sounds like Stewart screaming. What hair is Gus pointing that at?

That is definitely a drill and that is definitely Gail begging him to stop. This is sick. I bang madly on the door. "Gus, stop! You're crossing a line, Gus. What are you doing?! STOP!"

I'd rather not hang about. I open the cupboards looking for something heavy enough to break the double glazing – a casserole pot, a fire extinguisher, a Scottie dog door-stop. I settle for a kitchen chair. I time my thwacks with his torture episodes. Why draw attention to myself if I can help it? The window is above the sink, keeping me too far away to get enough force behind the chair. Out of breath, I sit down. What the fuck am I doing? Knocking my pan in to escape is tantamount to telling Gus he's the big guy, telling him he's running the show when actually, he's pitiful. Gus is the shit on my shoe. I will sit here with my dignity and party with the schmuck when he comes back.

Gus would give anything not to need the respect of the others. It bothers him that he wants the acceptance of such unremarkable specimens. He hates himself for it and he hates them for it too, so they have to die. He won't kill me though. He's not ashamed of wanting my approval because it's worth having. Anyone would want to be more like me. He'll keep me alive to learn from me.

The morning room noises are hard to take. The only thing I know off-by-heart is a hymn from school assembly. I sing about a green hill far away at the top of my voice.

The oven clock says seventeen minutes have passed when the kitchen door opens. He doesn't take me to the morning room. Keeps me where I am. He's not all here, if you know what I mean. In some psychopathic frenzy that is probably making total sense to him. Turning on the cooker rings and plugging in the coffee grinder will be fitting with a logic I have no hope of penetrating. Gun in hand, he fiddles with the end of a roll of cellophane, which he manages to free, and wraps it round and round

146

my torso, cling-filming me to the seat. Then he places a chair opposite me and sits wielding the gun with a maniacal grimace.

I open with a casual ice-breaker, "Isn't it so often the way? You take the time to make your whole house look nice, and then people spend all evening hanging around in the kitchen."

"Tell me you like my new Insignia."

"Gus..."

"Ask me about it! Ask me about engine size."

"For Christ's sake, it's a Vauxhall."

"A coupé, though. Unbelievable traction. Sexy, isn't it? Isn't it!"

"You have the dogs of a man who has no balls and the car of a man with no personality."

Maybe I'll be in this chair for hours more or maybe it'll be over in minutes. Either way I don't seem to care. It's not 'life' that is important, it's quality of life; "So what if your house has been repossessed / wife has left you for a younger man / mother isn't your real mother / business partner did a runner – so what? You're *alive*, that's what matters." Fuck that philosophy. Who would want to be alive after any of that? Living with public humiliation isn't living. A small, compromised existence isn't worth having. If you're doing things properly, you play to win. It's a damage limitation exercise – ding ding, round two, play it, fight for it, score the point. The other guy only cares about himself and you should too. Concede and you're lost. People who crumble and crumple – I can't stand those people.

"How's your golf handicap these days, Monty? Still in the twenties?" he asks.

"Gus, you're stalling. Whatever you're in here to do get on with it. If it's a build-up in tension you're trying to

147

achieve, frankly, I'm bored. It's been a long evening. Let's move it along. If you really want to, we could do a preliminary half hour of forehead on the hotplate and fingers in the coffee-grinder and then you could kill me with a bullet. I mean, whatever you think is the best way to proceed. All I'm saying is, if it's the satisfaction of me screaming and begging for mercy you're after, it's not going to happen. Just so you know. In case that makes a difference to your timetable. Will you stop staring at me! Jesus. It's making me waffle."

He places the end of the gun right against my temple and, no word of a lie, I don't flinch. I don't expel a bead of sweat or tense a single muscle. I could be a drunk on a night bus. Seconds pass, maybe a minute.

"Monty, goddamn," Gus shouts, "you're impossible! OK, hell, I give in. I'm not going to kill you. I haven't killed anyone. They screamed on cue and then snuck away with their headlights off." Gus's face has reverted back to its own smarmy version of normal. So stunned by this complete change in atmosphere, I'm not sure I heard him correctly. "What are you talking about?"

"I'm talking about Helen," he answers. "She phoned me yesterday. She was upset. Said you'd gone on and on at her until she caved and agreed not to come. Well, let me tell you, that seat at my table is Helen's. She is our dear friend. You are the overweening sod we have put up with because, for reasons known only to her, Helen liked you."

"We?"

"Yes, all of us. We've tolerated you but I can't say anyone was disappointed to hear about the break-up. Jubilant might better describe it."

I am so tired – a post-adrenaline crash. "What a song and dance, Gus. Can you get me out of this plastic? Why didn't you just phone me and give me an earful? Tell me I wasn't welcome?"

"This was much more fun, don't you think? A bit of a practical joke *extraordinaire*. Where's the satisfaction in a phone call with Mr Supercilious Smart Alec?"

Gus points a pair of scissors at my neck, places them astride the cellophane casing and cuts his way down. I despair that he cared that much about making his point, and thought his scheme was funny enough, to go to all that effort. All I can utter is, "I need to leave now."

He unlocks the kitchen and we walk down the hall. I feel no relief walking out the front door. I feel like a low-life: their protective love for Helen being healthier than anything I could ever offer. On the doorstep, I say, "Well, it's good to know you all dislike me as much I do you."

Gus holds his car key up, asking, "Run you home?"

"In that thing? Nah. I'd rather walk."

About the author

Kate Tough's first novel, *When You Kill a Thing and It Doesn't Die*, was awarded a Scottish Arts Council bursary and short-listed for the CPP women's fiction prize. It´s being published in 2013. Kate was selected for the prestigious *26 Treasures* exhibition at the National Museum of Scotland in 2011-12, and her poem is in the *26 Treasures* collection, published by Unbound. Since gaining a Masters in Creative Writing, Kate has taught in professional and community settings. In 2009, she was writer-in-residence at the Wigtown Book Festival (a festival she highly recommends). Kate is the host of Glasgow 's monthly showcase, *Poetry@The Ivory*.

www.katetough.com

Rat Trap

Paula R C Readman

If you are asking me if I believe in forgiveness, in my experience, those who beg for mercy, seldom deserve it.

Last night was difficult for me. In the end, I turned over onto my back in bed, eager to find rest, when somewhere outside my room a door slammed and robbed me of my sleep once more. For some reason sleep eluded me. Under normal circumstances I sleep well, even better after the excitement of a kill. Although I always believe it's the smell of the blood that helped me to sleep.

But not tonight.

For the first time in years, I haven't slept well. Eventually, I had to get up and switch on the light.

And here you are? Like some half-forgotten dream.

Questions, bloody questions. If you are going to rob me of my sleep tonight, I might as well answer your questions. To start with, you really need to sort out the lighting in this place. It's too dull.

Oh, so you're telling me the lighting is supposed to calm my nerves. Lady, the last thing you should worry about are my nerves. What's puzzling me though is why you're wandering about at this time of night, anyway. Can't you sleep? Or maybe you've something to hide too!

Questions more bloody questions.

So what's with wanting to know about my mother now?

I might as well tell you, I suppose. Overall, she was a good woman, maybe a little bossy. Really, I don't know about other people's mothers. Where I lived separated me from the rest of the community... Now look here, others like you, might view my isolation as being wrong, but for me it made things easier. Mum was a qualified teacher, who opted to do my schooling at home, as the nearest schools were many miles away. Mum liked living alone, especially after Dad left, though, she liked to drive to the nearest church every Sunday.

Originally, my family weren't church-going folks until after we moved to the new house.

What! You think I'm making excuses for my behaviour. Let me tell you, lady you've got it so wrong!

With pride, Mum told me, "We're God-fearing people, Aaron. I want everyone to know we're living the way the Good Lord expects us to live."

And Lord, didn't I know it.

Every day and night, she made me get down on my knees and pray. Just a quick prayer for world peace wasn't good enough for my mum. No, she had a long list of things we had to pray for, and last on that list was my dear old dad. I did wonder whether she hoped he'd return, but I knew that was impossible. She was fond of telling me, "No matter what you do, my son, God will always forgive you and wash away your sins." I felt she had some funny ideas about God and his infinite powers. Telling me 'He' worked in mysterious ways, as if I believed in all that shit. I suppose I was about twelve when I realised I wasn't like other boys.

God, I could do with a drink, right now. Do you want one?

I can see you're surprised that I've got a secret stash. You'd be amazed to know how we inmates manage to get things brought in here. This isn't a prison, you know. Though, I prefer my whiskey in a glass to a plastic beaker.

You say I shouldn't drink as it brings out the worst in me. That's something else my mother would've agreed with you on, "The devil's brew that's what drink is!" she would holler at my father. So I guess it's lucky, she's not here, with us then.

Whiskey was my dear old dad's favourite tipple, but Mum never let him enjoy it in peace. I raise my glass to him and hope he's found the peace he craved for so much. He'd spend most of his time out in the woods rather than at home with us. We were lucky, I suppose, where we lived. Surrounded on three sides by trees, our house once belonged to Mum's family. It stood at the end of an old farm track, overlooking a large lake. I remember, with perfect clarity, when we first drove up the winding drive the day after Mum received the keys to her inheritance. Dad was over the moon at the sight of the lake. He thought every day would be a fishing day for him now that they had a good bit of money tucked away for a rainy day. Dad hoped he could reduce his working hours and finally start to enjoy his life once more, but Mum had other plans. All too soon he realised he wasn't going to live his dream, but pay for ours.

He began to skulk out of the house, through the garden, and then out into the woods. Sometimes, unbeknown to him, I would follow him like a ghost. It soon became my favourite game. Laughing to myself, I would hide among the undergrowth unseen and unheard. From there, I could see the look of fear growing in his tired eyes as he stumbled and staggered through the wood, occasionally glancing back over his shoulder, trying to see who or what was following him.

Deep within the woods, he had built himself a sanctuary in the shape of a log cabin. Here he had all he needed. In one corner of the hut, stood a small, old pot-belly stove in which Dad burnt the magazines and books Mum never allowed into the house. These weren't even the sort of magazines other people would see as being unsuitable reading material.

The change in my mother was staggering since we moved to the house; she discarded almost everything from our past life. The old armchair in Dad's bolt-hole had always been his, but now it wasn't good enough for our new house. Within his cabin, he read his forbidden books and magazines while slowly getting drunk, some nights he wouldn't even bother coming home. Shutting the door, he would sleep it off there until the early morning when he took a swim in the lake before returning home to a hearty breakfast. On my father's good days, he would get me to help him to cut logs for our fires and for selling as Dad had found the means of becoming his own boss, supporting us, and escaping the rat race. He would allow me to cut kindling for the kitchen stove. Watching me, with pride, he would smile and say what a good lad I was, which would make me smile back at him. The smell of the wood excited me almost as much as the weight of the axe in my hand and as for the sound of the axe slicing through the wood... thwack... made my mouth go dry, and as for what happened next... sweet, sweet... No, I must keep to my story. It's important to me, that I tell you in sequence so you can understand it all.

I always thought we were a close family. There was the three of us Dad, Mum, and me. Our perfect world, Mum called it as she took me up to my bed and tucked me in for the night. We never needed anyone else, but somehow moving to the new house changed everything. It saddens me to look back now, and remember all I've lost because of the move to that unforgiving house.

Yes, unforgiving.

Who said, a house couldn't be called unforgiving. Look lady, I don't have much time, so do you want to hear what I've got to say, or do you want to go now? It's up to you.

Right, back to the house, it is then. It was large and Gothic. The sort of house the writer, Stephen King adored, all dark and brooding. The sort of place that had a dark soul lurking within its eye-like windows, which had stood for centuries, watching and waiting as life's imperfections unfolded within its rooms and grounds. If the outside looked unwelcoming, then the inside was even less so. My dearly departed great aunt Livinia seemed to have adored everything morbid and depressing. The rooms seemed to close in and gave off sombre feelings. Every room was full of stuffed animals and birds as well as dark, heavy furniture, which made you feel like you were walking into a mausoleum instead of a house. It sucked the very life out of your bones, even my dad commented on it at the time, "Good God, Mary, I feel like I've come here to die. Well, I suppose once we get rid of those heavy old velvet curtains and you've put your magic touch to the house. It will feel less like our final resting place, and more like heaven on earth."

Mum smiled her beautiful smile, rolled her sleeves up and started to clean the old kitchen. As the days passed, the house began to shine. The smell of fresh paint filled the place along with our happiness. I'm not sure, what brought about the change to my happy childhood. I was more than happy to be the centre of my parent's world and remember so clearly the closeness I had with my father. How he used to ruffle my hair as he passed me by while I sat reading my comic or watching telly. That reminds me: Mum took exception to the television and suddenly didn't like us having one in the house. "What the hell's wrong with the telly, woman? A man's got to have some way of relaxing when he comes home after a hard day grafting," Dad shouted at her after finding her smashing up another set after he'd just replaced the last one.

I blamed my parents for what has happened to me, or was it the rat?

What do you think, Lady?

Oh, haven't I told you about the rat.

Well, if you're sitting comfortably then I shall begin. Once upon a time... that's so funny... are you sitting comfortably?

Anyway, about the rat. I was four at the time. Mum was busy painting, and dad, I think he may have been at work. I was happily wandering around when I heard a low pitiful, squeaking sound followed by a sort of clunk clunk noise in one of the outbuildings. So I went in to investigate. There in the centre of the floor was a big, brown rat, with horrid, yellow teeth, and a rattrap caught on its tail. It seemed so small and pathetic.

It was so funny I nearly wet myself laughing. Trapped between two large petrol cans, it couldn't go forward or backwards nor could it get to its tail to chew through it to release itself.

Can you imagine chewing through your own leg or wrist to free yourself, lady?

Hmm, I quite like the idea of watching someone so desperate to make such a choice.

Ha, if you could see your face now, it's a real picture.

Anyway, back to the rat. I poked it with a stick and it squealed. The sound was amazing. It made me buzz with energy. For once I was in control. It twisted and turned, clanking the trap against the side of the cans, but it wasn't going anywhere. It even tried going up the side of the cans, but the trap stopped and held it fast. Every time it stopped trying to escape and lay panting, I poked it again, sending it into a frenzy. It snarled and squealed madly. I felt liberated and free as young as I was. I had a sense of overwhelming power. And the fun was unbelievable.

155

After that, none of my other silly toys gave me as much pleasure as tormenting the rat did. I looked around for something else to poke it with as it kept gnawing at my stick. It bled from its mouth. The droplets of blood covered the cans and soaked its fur. In the end, I found my father's screwdriver and poked it as hard as I could. The blade slipped into it as a jet of hot blood shot out and covered my hand. The rat lay on its side twitching until it moved no more. Picking it up by the trap, I carried it outside and tossed it and the screwdriver into the stream before washing my hands.

Hmm, the rat, it's funny how when I look back everything seems so normal to me, but you, you make it seem so different.

Shall I go on?

One day, my parents had a bright idea to get me a puppy. They had some silly dreams of seeing me playing with a dog, of us going off together to explore the woods, just that silly little dog and me. Me, I had some plans of my own to play with that large, floppy-eared, doe-eyed pup. Lying in my bed early one morning my first thoughts was how to make the pleasure last longer than it had with the rat. As I lay thinking about it, my mouth and nose filled with the sweet taste of blood. Don't get me wrong, I don't drink the blood, that's too disgusting. It's the smell of it, it gets into your nose, and throat until you can taste it in your mouth. It's like the smell of fish and chips, it drives you crazy, and makes you want to go and buy some.

It's funny thinking about that stupid dog now. It was as if the mutt knew what I was going to do to it. It hid from me when I came down that morning. After breakfast, it took me an hour to find it. In the end, Dad brought it to me. He laughed at me and said, "I don't know what's wrong with the poor little thing, but it was pining for you." He handed its lead to me, and then ruffled my hair before turning and heading back indoors. He called back over his shoulder as he went, "Have a great day, my son, but don't be late home. You know, how your mother worries about you."

I could see fear in that mutt's eyes as though it could read my mind. It twisted and turned on its lead as though it would rather strangle itself than to let me have my fun.

Hey, lady I can see that same look in your eyes. Not to worry, I haven't finished my story yet.

What I can't understand is why my parents couldn't see that I was happy being on my own. Anyway, things came to a head when my baby brother, Pete, died. After that, Mum went to pieces.

Why was she so upset? I mean – she still had me.

I was six at the time. Mum was busy in the kitchen cooking our dinner and Dad lay stretched out in the parlour with the telly on loud, when Pete started to bawl. Mum had only just fed him, and it was time for his nap, so she shouted to Dad to look at him for her. I heard Dad shout something back, but Mum didn't hear him. So I crept along the hallway to his nursery and pushed the door open.

Mum regularly told me how lucky I was to have a baby brother. I couldn't see it myself. But she insisted I would enjoy taking him fishing when he was old enough. She even said, I would never be lonely again. I never saw myself as being lonely with just the three of us. As though, I wanted to take him with me while I went out to play my games. I hated him. I liked being on my own, to be able to play my special games whenever I wanted to. What fun could I have with a shitty little baby? I had one game I wanted to play with him, but I knew I had to wait until the right time.

157

And, this was that time. As I stepped into the room, he started to whimper like the puppy with its lead pulled too tight and then I saw that same puppy look in my baby brother's eyes. It was as though all the wisdom in the world was born within him but he couldn't use it until he grew up enough to understand the words to call out for help. His eyes seemed to follow me around the room as though he understood quite clearly what I was about to do to him. Was he able to read my mind, I wondered? Well, if he could make them understand just what he wanted by crying and stopping them from doing what they wanted to do, then to me, it seemed I should be the one to set them free from his control. After all four was too many.

There was no fun in it; it was far too easy, and far too clean. I held his stupid brown teddy bear; the one Mum said I had brought for him, when he first came into our house, to his wet, whimpering face. After a moment, he stopped moving. Using the stool, I placed it back on the shelf where Mother said he could see it. Of course, I always put things back as I find them, well, almost everything, apart from the crying baby.

I closed the door behind me and went back to my room. Soon Mum called us to the dinner table. She had dished ours up while she went to see to Pete. Her scream sometimes haunts me during the night, especially when I don't have a good kill. It's the sort of scream which travels through your body and tears at your soul. It's a scream which tells you someone or something was dying inside. There isn't any escape from the hell they've found themselves in and everyone around must hear their pain and share in their suffering.

Covering my ears, I tried to shut it out. I couldn't understand why she was screaming, hadn't I shut the bloody thing up. After all that's what Dad had said when Mum had called to him. "Can't you shut the kid up? I'm trying to watch the telly."

The police came, then the ambulance. The house seemed to suck everyone in, until it was full of people asking questions. I thought about the rat, when I saw Pete's white coffin carried out. Everyone called me, the poor little mite, and was nice to me, trying to make me smile by ruffling my hair. A woman kindly asked me if I helped my mummy to look after the baby. I said, "Mummy did not like me touching the new baby. She said I played too rough, but I'm good at playing on my own."

A puzzled look crossed her face, and then she scribbled something in her notebook. I smiled at her and she hugged me, telling me not to worry, Pete had gone to a better place. I couldn't see that myself, but I didn't tell her that. Suddenly, I felt uneasy about everything. I decided I did not like this game anymore and I wasn't going to play.

Pete's death unhinged my mother. She blamed herself for not going to check on him when he stopped crying, she'd already started to blame Dad for watching too much telly and not spending enough time with his children. The police hadn't made it any easier for them as a child's death always pointed the finger of suspicion at the parents first. Later there was talk about Mum not being fit enough to look after me either.

Mum started to take me to church after Pete's death. In the church was a statue of the suffering Christ. He stared down at me every Sunday, his arms outstretched and blood soaked hands. Mother told me it wasn't blood, but the sins of the world. But I knew it was just red paint. I adored the statue's face with its look of pure agony. It was the same look, I saw on my father's face as I brought down the axe.... Thwack... and took off his hand. From his kneeling position, he crumpled and stared up at me with the same questioning look of why, as though he saw someone other than me standing over him. Oh, how richly the bright, red blood sparkled in the afternoon sun, and flowed like the stream after the heavy, summer rain.

It's funny, how the little things stick in your mind. My father's hand lay where it fell and within its palm, a pool of blood gathered. His wedding ring glistened with a ring of blood as his life force ebbed away from him. I don't know why, but I'd thought it would've lain there twitching like the rat and the puppy after I'd ripped its throat out. I even wondered if Pete would've done the same.

Dad moaned softly and held on to his bleeding wrist as he begged for help. Taking the axe, I began to hack at his throat. At first, he raised his good hand in a feeble protest, but I ignored him, closing my eyes I continued to hack at him. When I stopped and stepped back to look at my handy work, I was pleased and excited. It was much better than the rat and even the dog. I remembered what the vicar had said in the Sunday service about seeing the light. Well, I could honestly say at that point in my life. I had seen the light, I was ten and this was the best game ever.

I had made a bit of a mess, but that didn't bother me. Dad was fond of saying how good I was at tidying up after I had been playing. Even though we were deep within the woods, I didn't think it was a good idea just to leave Dad lying about. Most of all, it looked untidy. I was, as Dad said, a bit on the scrawny side. He liked to tell Mum that I needed building up, which is why he brought me here to chop wood with him.

Standing in the fading afternoon light, I looked about for a way to tidy up my mess. I wasn't strong enough to dig a hole or to drag Dad to the lake. I began to laugh when the idea hit me. Mohammed may have gone to the mountain, but I wasn't about to, I was far smarter than that, I brought it to me. After rolling Dad a couple of feet up against the log pile, I began to cover him in logs.

There was only one time Mum had come to the woods to see what Dad was going on about when he told her about his plans to make and sell charcoal and other by products from the woods. She had commented about Dad's log pile then, saying there was more than enough to last us a lifetime. In Dad's case, she was right.

All through the Church services, I would stare at the statue. My dear mum dreamt of me becoming a priest because she thought I understood Christ's suffering. She liked to tell the congregation that it was a painting, which hung in my bedroom, set me on my road to Damascus. I laughed behind her back. Oh yes, I had found enlightenment from the painting especially when the moonlight shone through the gap in my curtains and highlighted the pained face of Christ. It aroused such excitement in me; at first, I was too young to understand the pleasure I found when I woke to see his suffering and pained expression. All I knew was I liked it a lot.

Of course, Mum had to go next. She had become a little tiresome. At first, she was angry with my father for clearing off and leaving me alone for days in the woods. A police officer, who had also been one of Dad's customers, found me wandering about covered in dirt and soaking wet. They dragged the lake looking for Dad's body or even any sign of him. They questioned me, but I had learnt to be a bit vague and once again that paid off. Soon he was forgotten, and it wasn't as though Mum had many friends asking her unanswered questions about

Dad's disappearance, and as for me, I never had any friends.

Now there was the two of us.

Somehow, my happy home had lost its sparkle. Mum locked herself away in her bedroom for days on end, leaving me to look after myself. This was the first time I was able to explore the house on my own. I couldn't begin to tell you how exciting it was to come across the cellar. It was large and spacious. Single light bulbs dotted about giving off ghostly shadows among the discarded broken furniture and boxes. Shining my torch about, I made my way between them. Deep within the cellar, I found a small, windowless room. Turning off my torch, I stood in the darkness and inhaled deeply. I was twelve now, and feared nothing and no one, not even the darkness. Over the last two years, I had shot up in height and put on weight, I had even taken up running to build up my stamina.

Switching my torch back on, I stood casting the beam around as I tried to think of a way to get Mum to come down here. I knew one thing for sure; she had a fear of the darkness. Getting my mother to enter the cellar of her own freewill wouldn't be easy. If I had learnt one thing in my short life, fear and darkness are a deadly combination to most people; to me it was a thing of fascination.

Call it fate, or the luck of the Gods, but the problem was taken out of my hands. If there was one thing my mother feared more than the darkness, it was having no power in the house. Having no television, papers or radio, we had no idea about the storm which was about to hit the country. The first we knew was when the wind brought down a tree and the lights began to flicker. I was in my bedroom reading when a light knock came at my door.

"Come in."

"Aaron, what's wrong with the lights."

"It's probably just the storm, Mum, nothing to worry about. It will soon pass," I said casually, showing no interest in her.

She stepped away from the door, coming further into my room. "I wish your father was here." Her voice shook as she spoke.

I looked up. For the first time in years, she spoke about Dad. There she sat at the end of my bed with her hands covering her ears and rocking backwards and forwards. Outside, the wind and rain gave forth a torrent of wailing and pounding against the house. Inside, the flickering lights danced in time with the wind and rain.

She turned her ashen face to me, "Isn't there anything we can do to stop the lights from flickering. It's driving me crazy."

"We could check the fuses," I said, closing my book.

"Oh, yes, of course, the fuses. I'm not sure where the fuse box is?"

Laying my book on the bed, I said, "In the cellar, I suppose."

How sweet was that? I smiled into the beautiful darkness as the lights flickered again.

Now dressed in her jeans and a large fluffy jumper, Mum hesitated at the top of the cellar stairs. Below her, the low wattage light bulbs danced in time with the raging storm.

"Do we have to go down there?" her voice questioning, like a frightened child.

"Yes, but it'll be all right, you have me. There's nothing to be afraid of."

She patted my hand. "I know, I was so lucky with you. You've always been so strong, so self-contained, and

163

seemed to know what you wanted."

For a moment her comment puzzled me, but the smile on her face softened the lines around her mouth and I dismissed it. Picking up my torch, I shone it into the darkness as Mum followed behind. Carefully, I helped her pick her way between the broken chairs and discarded rubbish boxes.

"I should've got your father to clear this place out years ago," Mum said as we went deeper into the darkness. Behind us, the sound of the storm faded. Reaching out, she stopped and peered into one of the boxes. "I wonder..." she said, her voice steady as though she had forgotten about our reason for being down here.

"It's not far now," I said, my excitement growing. I stepped behind her, smelling her fear. Had it really been so long since my last kill? I could feel my hands shaking.

"I don't think we need to be down here," she said her voice surprisingly steady.

"What?" Shocked, I caught her in the torchlight she turned to face me.

Her face marked by age and uncertainty, seemed to take on a look of reverence. "I remember now, the fuse box isn't down here."

"It is here," I said sharply and pointed the torchlight in front of me. "It's just a bit further on." The darkness sucked at us as the next light bulb swung slightly in a ring of dust particles.

"No!" Mum snapped. The single word held all her lost strength and self-belief, "it's in the kitchen."

As she pushed past me, I slid the knife between her ribs.

She stopped. Her hand dropped to her side. I smiled into her puzzled face.

"Why?" Her voice trembled and seemed to reflect the

164

puzzlement on her face as though some long forgotten memory had returned in that fleeting moment.

I thought she was asking about the knife, but then I realised she wasn't.

"How did you know?"

She looked down at her hands now covered in blood. "I saw you enter his room, Aaron. He was so small, so vulnerable…" Her voice trailed off. "Why? I had enough love for both of you." Her breath weakened.

"Love?" I laughed. "It has nothing to do with loving me. I did it because I could, and because no one stopped me."

She slipped down the side of the box. I leaned over her. "Why didn't you say something while you had the chance, Mother?"

But she was gone.

Most people blame their mother for their own failings, not me. For me, it was the stupid rat! After all this time, it was most annoying. I've always been careful, never staying too long in one place, especially after a kill. I carefully selected vulnerable people, who were in a desperate need of a friend, or someone who cared enough to listen to them. I learnt that from my good friend, Jesus, you know. Only I didn't bother with the 'do unto others as you wish done unto you' crap. You'll be surprised just how many sad, lonely people there are around you in your everyday life. You pass them in the street; you may even work with them. They are grey nondescript sort of people who show no emotion or enthusiasm for life until unexpectedly it is about to be taken from them. Then, wow, you'll be amazed about how much they want to live, suddenly life takes on a new meaning and they come alive.

You want to know why I kill them. It's because it's the reason for my existence and I don't see why I should forget all about my pleasure, and my enjoyment because they've suddenly, after a few days with me, experiencing my world, and my game, have found a reason to continue living their sad, little lives.

No, I've a lot to thank my parents for, if it wasn't for them I wouldn't have found my true path in life. Take my looks, a picture of innocence. It's helped me in my chosen career, you might say. Women adored me and men trusted me. With my soft boyish looks, fair hair and skin, with sparkling blue eyes I make them feel especially loved. There's been too many now and every one of them, I've given all they've desired: love and understanding. In return they give me life.

It took me weeks, months or even a year of careful planning, to set the scene for my game of make-believe. With an added new dimension to my game, I take photographs. In the past, my only way of reliving it, was in dreams, but now I can replay it as many times as I want to. The pictures tell their own stories of our fun days out, in the park, on beaches, and at the funfair, not forgetting their smiling, happy faces alive with life itself.

The rooms I rented, I set the scenes to show off my photographs of a happier time of just the three of us, Mum, Dad, and me. When they tell me how wonderful their life has become, and they trust me. Just like God, I snatch their perfect life away. The first they know of it, is an unexpected blow to the side of the neck. Thank God, I gave up the axe, it's far too messy.

Then deep, within the dark basement, among the discarded rubbish, my sleeping beauty awakes to find she's locked away in a new world of shadows. After weeks of indulging her, it's time for her to play my game. I

166

understand her confusion, like all the rest before her. What I long to see is the fear within their eyes. It heightens my excitement as they give me back the pleasure I've given to them. It's that 'do unto others' scenario.

I make them suffer, watching as the little light of their life goes out slowly, and desperation takes over. It's like finding the trapped rat of my childhood again. In my experience, those who beg for mercy seldom deserve it.

They gnawed at the ropes that bind their wrists, in the same way you're doing now, Doctor. It's funny, that it's tonight of all nights, you should have come to me with your questions.

My mind races when I think about my last and final pleasure as I called her, though, I didn't know it at the time. If it hadn't been for that bloody rat appearing like magic, from under an old, Gothic wardrobe, I could've continued my game. It stood facing me, sniffing the air as though it could already smell blood, before disappearing back from whence it came.

The strongest of them all, she hadn't begged for mercy, like the rest. Just lying there, she watched me with large, blue, knowing eyes. She fascinated me with her endurance. My mistake was forgetting about the game. I even wondered if I was losing my touch, becoming too cocky in my old age, twenty-six, and still enjoying my childhood games.

Like the rat, she was far cleverer than I had realised, bided her time and mine too. Had she known the old wardrobe hid a doorway? The bloody rat brought her, her freedom and the police to my door after a pest-controller broke through from the neighbour's cellar and found her locked in mine.

Now it's your turn, Doctor Newton. You came to me,

with questions about my game. So why not experience the pleasure here within my dull, clinical, white room. I'm sorry I hope the strips of sheets aren't too tight. How I wish there was more time to make you comfortable, but at least, we can have some fun.

She stares up at me with wide, green eyes as I slip the first needle in under her fingernail. For a moment, I wonder just how long it would take her to start begging me for mercy as I slip in the second.

About the author

Paula R. C. Readman lives in a small Essex village, with her husband, Russell and son, Stewart . *Rat Trap* is her third published short story. English Heritage published her first in 2010: *Whitby Abbey-Pure Inspiration*. In 2011, she was the overall winner in the World Book Day short story competition, run by Austin and Macauley Publishers, and was the overall winner in the Writing Magazine Harrogate Crime Competition 2012 when the best-selling crime writer Mark Billingham picked her short dark crime story *Roofscapes*. In addition, Paula has had several nonfiction articles published. With special thanks to Russell and Stewart as well as all her family and friends for their kind words encouragement especially, Joan , Bex, Ana , Linda and author Elizabeth (Ivy) Lord.

Catch up with Paula on facebook and her blog at
http://darkfantasy13writer.blogspot.co.uk

The Courgette House

Stephen Puleston

"I've never begged for mercy and never will."

Frankie Long tipped a water bottle to his lips and swallowed hard. He brushed away the perspiration gathering on his forehead as three pairs of eyes stared at him, waiting. He shifted his position on a small wooden box, trying to make himself comfortable

By his side Mickey French stifled a yawn tugging at his jaw; he'd heard it all before. Terry Welsh and Stan Haddock exchanged nervous glances and in the few days since starting in the courgette house had learned never to interrupt Frankie.

"The trouble with the criminal justice system is that the true criminals never get their just deserts," Frankie continued.

"Yes, of course, Boss," Mickey said.

Welsh and Haddock sipped on their water bottles.

They sat listening to Frankie's justification for the assault that led to his conviction, agreeing when appropriate and occasionally nodding encouragement. Behind them boxes full of courgettes were piled on trolleys along the concrete path that dissected the two acre greenhouse filled with flowering green plants. Some were young with flowers still clinging to the fruit, others over-ripe, the size of marrows.

Then Frankie told them about Locatelli.

"I hate Italians."

More nodding.

"You're not Italian are you?"

Headshaking.

"He thought he was the Mafia. Moving in on my patch."

169

Mickey's voice broke in, "But you'll show him won't you, Boss?"

"Only a matter of time. And when he begs for mercy. Well..."

Mickey snorted, Welsh and Haddock grunted an encouraging response.

Then they heard footsteps approaching and two prison officers appeared in the doorway.

"Busy I see lads," the taller said.

The shorter officer, with no neck and hands like shovels, looked at Frankie. "Probation wants to see you."

Frankie nodded and retrieving his prison-issue striped shirt headed towards the main administration block. He was pleased to be leaving the stifling heat of the courgette house and for a break from the monotony of the prison regime. The screws strode out in front until they reached the administration wing and left Frankie pushing open the double-doors.

A prisoner mopping the floors nodded an acknowledgment of respect to Frankie as he made his way through the corridors. He reached a door that had a narrow metal sign with the name of the duty officer in plastic letters. There was a muffled response when he knocked and he pushed open the door. The atmosphere was stifling and the air second-hand – he wondered how anyone could work in there. The probation officer was a short woman with a severe haircut and a silver nose ring. A small fan that sat alongside the telephone on her desk turned intermittently sending a weak blast of air that moved a couple of hairs hanging over her ears.

"Prisoner Long, sit down."

She was formal, no first names, no eye contact. A green coloured folder was open on her desk, a pile of buff and red folders piled untidily in a corner. Frankie had sat in the same seat a dozen times when she'd been preparing her report for the parole board and he'd barely given a second thought to the platitudes that had fallen from his lips.

"I've got the parole board's decision."

Frankie wasn't expecting the decision for another week. He clasped the fingers of both hands into a fist and felt his lips drying.

"Good news," she lifted her eyes.

Slowly, he unclasped his fists and smiled at her.

Outside Frankie stood in the summer sunshine. The sky was cloudless and a brilliant blue colour. He could smell the cut grass and the flowers in the borders. He was going to be free of this place. He was going to be able to walk into his home and kiss his wife and hug his grandchildren.

The news travelled quickly. Screws nodded at him and their eyes told him they knew. Frankie tried a smile when one told him not to come back. He walked round the open prison with more confidence, more of a jaunt. After lock-up he lay on his bed, staring at the ceiling.

Thinking.

Within an hour of Frankie Long opening his fists and smiling at the probation officer a fax landed on the desk of Detective Inspector Jamie McPherson. He read it twice, made three telephone calls, sat back in his chair before deciding that he had to have a cigarette.

He walked through the musty corridors of the police station turning over in his mind the snippets from informants. The cash and carry robbery was still unsolved and establishing Locatelli's guilt had been impossible, but the whispers told him Frankie had been double-crossed. McPherson stood outside a rear door and took a cigarette from the crumpled packet in his jacket. He dragged long and hard, letting the smoke fill his lungs. It had been three years ago since he had sat in court and watched Frankie's face as the judge sentenced him – not a flicker of remorse, no emotion, just that look of a professional facing the consequences.

McPherson couldn't shake off the feeling gnawing at his mind that Frankie's reputation meant a score had to be settled.

On the morning of his release Frankie ignored the apprehension that crept into his mind. Mickey French gave him a man hug as he left the billet that had been his home and Frankie promised to keep in touch.

The formalities of checking belongings, signing declarations and counting the discharge grant dragged. He got up and walked round the room to curb his irritation at the banter from the young prisoners, excited at the prospect of release.

Once the processing was over Frankie stepped out into the summer sunshine, the warmth massaging his face. He closed his eyes and tilted his head skywards. Fresh air and sunshine tasted different for a free man.

"Frankieee…" the voice got louder and he saw Madge her arms in the air running towards him

She threw herself at him and he felt the warmth of her body against his. Frankie curled his hand round Madge's waist and squeezed. The flesh was soft but more expansive then he remembered. He squeezed her hand as they walked to the car. On the journey home the traffic seemed heavier and faster than he remembered. They stopped at a services and Frankie stared at the choice of food available until a girl behind the counter with a sullen stare said, "Well do you want anything?"

He tried to hide the easiness in his mind – it had been three years since he'd been a free man. He looked her in the eye and ordered. She spooned the food into a plate and he sat down. Watching people walking through the services he noticed women with prams, an elderly couple with grandchildren tugging at their arms and a line of foreign tourists buying gifts at a checkout. Unlike the last three years nobody paid him any attention.

He smiled to himself – he was free once more.

Three hours after his release Frankie put a can of lager down on the cabinet by the side of the bed and gazed over at Madge.

"Frankie, it's been so long." There was a nervous tone to her voice.

He looked over at her as she unfastened her trousers and wiggling her hips let the material fall to the floor. Had he been twenty years younger he would have torn her clothes off before they'd closed the front door.

"I know I've put on weight," she said.

He stepped towards her and undid her bra.

"Madge, you're still my babe."

Afterwards, he lay in the warmth of the bed and pulled Madge close drawing his hand through her hair. Her skin felt smooth and warm against his body and her breath tickled the hairs on his chest.

"Frankie, we need to get ready," Madge said eventually slipping out of bed. After a shower, he unwrapped a new shirt and pulled on a pair of grey trousers. He rummaged through a drawer, finding a gold necklace, a gift from Peter's wife Sophie, and hung it round his neck; on his wrist sat a gold band, a gift from Madge and on each hand he had gold rings – gifts from the grandchildren. He looked at himself in the mirror. Three years in various prisons and he'd lost two stone in weight, three inches around the waist and, whenever he looked in the mirror, there were too many grey hairs for comfort.

"I look like a Christmas turkey."

"What's wrong Frankie?" Madge said sitting by her dressing table, carefully plucking her eyebrows and turning her face to either side as if convincing herself the double chin wasn't showing. "You always liked the gifts from the family."

He let his hands fall to his side and dismissed his worries as the embers of post-release blues.

The Crippled Bear had a selection of eight cask conditioned ales, ten lagers, including a cloudy wheat variety from Belgium, and so many soft drinks Frankie's mind fizzed from the choices. He had known Arfon forever. It felt like a hundred years. Arfon had a thin narrow frame with legs like a butcher's dog but a stomach that hung out over the waistband of his trousers held up by a belt tightened at a rakish angle round his body. He smiled at Frankie exposing a row of teeth tarnished yellow by years of nicotine. He coughed and a deep crackling sound, like dry wood on a roaring fire.

"Good to see you, Frankie."

He grasped Frankie's hand.

"And you."

"You all right?" he stepped backward and looked at Frankie. "There's nothing fucking left of you. All skin and bones."

Frankie thumped him on the arm.

"Get me a drink."

Frankie sipped from his favourite ale and let the warm bitter sensation grip his throat. Arfon stood by his side and grabbed his shoulder.

"So what are your plans?"

Frankie raised an eyebrow.

"Retire that's what you should do. Dig up the drug money and retire. You should keep out of trouble."

Frankie didn't respond and from the door he heard a scream and turning saw two of his three grandchildren. Becky and Rachel ran up, clutched his legs, and then inspected his jewellery, carefully turning them in their small fingers. Peter and Sophie followed their daughters. Sophie leaned over, her kisses brushed his cheeks.

"Nice to see you again. How are you?"

"Great, Love."

Danny was hiding behind his father's legs staring at the floor.

"Danny," Frankie began ruffling his grandson's hair.

The steak was medium rare and as the flavour of the meat assaulted Frankie's taste buds, accustomed to prison food, unseasoned and cooked to death, he became uncharacteristically silent. He looked up and caught the glances of his family as he finished the food before the others had barely started. He piled more chips onto his plate and beamed at Madge.

In the taxi home Frankie grabbed Madge as though he were a teenager again only to find her pushing him away.

"Behave," she said.

Later, at home Madge lay in his arms beneath the sheets, the bedroom air cool against their faces.

"It's good to have you back," Madge said.

She reached an arm across his shoulder.

"It's good to be home. Enjoyed tonight."

"You were enjoying that food."

Frankie thought about the thin red streak of blood on his plate.

"Nothing like a good steak."

"I do love you, Frankie," she pressed her arms tight around his body.

"Love you too."

"You won't get it any more trouble will you?"

"What at my age? Don't want to die in prison."

Two of the letters on the neon sign were broken and faded red patches on the door and the evidence of touch-up painting completed the tired appearance of the snooker club.

Frankie pulled open the door and took the stairs two at a time, reminding himself he had to maintain the training regime he adopted in prison. Fluorescent tubes covered the room in a pale glow, the smell of spilled beer and stale clothes filled the air. A dozen snooker tables all covered with black plastic sheets lined the room. He heard the tinkling of stacking glasses and bottles crashing against each other and turned towards the bar. A face appeared and two clear blue eyes looked over at Frankie, unmoved by his presence, as though he were expected.

"He's in the office," the man said.

Frankie nodded and walked over to the far end of the room, noticing the man's unwavering stare.

Peter got up from the leather bound chair behind the mahogany reproduction desk.

"Alright, Dad."

"What's wrong with the guy cleaning the bar?"

"Simple. He understands fuck all."

"Good."

Frankie curled his lips into a smile that said it's-good-to-be-back. He sat in the chair folding his arms behind his head, lifting his feet and rested them on the edge of the desk as he leaned back in the chair. Against one wall was a display cupboard with a selection of spirits. A small window cast a dull shadow across a leather Chesterfield whose arms needed attention.

"Locatelli," Frankie let the name hang in the air like an aged aunt's fart at a birthday party.

Peter cleared his throat.

"Don't you think it's time to forget about him?"

"You must be joking."

"But you want to move on. For Mum's sake."

"He's moved to Altrincham," Peter said, a resigned tone to his voice. "One of those gated communities."

Frankie jerked his feet off the desk and pulled the chair towards the desk. Peter continued.

"I heard he got shit-scared when you got parole. Hasn't been out. Takeaway pizzas left by the gate. CCTV cameras installed."

"What a shame," Frankie snorted. "We need to make plans."

Frankie's Mercedes passed the Bell and Anchor that stood on the corner of Mack Street and then swept down over the cobbles and occasional tarmac until it stopped by the lock-up underneath the railway arch. The street filled with the noise of a commuter train rattling over the points above. He powered down the window and sat back enjoying freedom, the smell of decaying rubbish and feline urine, being able to drive around Manchester, see his grandchildren, drinking with Arfon, and feeling the warmth of Madge by his side in the morning.

And, see to Locatelli.

It had been two long, hot summers in the courgette house since the deal with Paolo Locatelli had gone sour. Not a single day had passed without Frankie waking to the contemplation of Locatelli's fate. A warm damp smell hit

177

his nostrils and he remembered the launderette on the next street. As he glanced at his watch he saw his son's car turning into the street. Frankie was already outside the Mercedes when Peter drew up, stepped out and bleeped his car.

"You sure about this?" Peter said.

"Course."

"If the cops find out…"

"They won't."

Frankie heaved open the door of the lock-up, making enough space for them both to enter. The light from the torch in his left hand darted over the empty walls until it found the light switch.

"Wonderful," Frankie said as the bulb flickered into life

There was a table with boxes of car parts and some electronic switches. In a corner, at the far end, was a Belfast sink under a tap on a pipe jutting out of the wall.

"Just like I remember."

"What did you do…?" Peter's question trailed.

"When I started out I made a few bob from this place."

Frankie dragged a single wooden chair into the middle and placed it underneath the light.

"Perfect."

Frankie never liked Altrincham, too new-money for him, not enough bling and too many beauty parlours and hair stylists promising miraculous transformations. He drove past the entrance to The Beeches and slowed as he watched the gates open and a Porsche 911 slip out. He saw the first house behind the closing gate with its flickering alarm and manicured garden.

He imagined Locatelli enjoying fresh pasta and sipping a fine Chianti, all paid for with his money. He drew the car into the curb and watched the gate closing. He wrapped his fingers over the steering wheel, a light rain fell and the blades swished automatically, clearing the windscreen. The mobile rang and he saw Peter's number on the screen.

"Dad, where are you?"

"Altrincham."

"You're not…"

"Yeah. Lovely isn't it?"

Their conversation was stilted, Peter tried persuasion and then an appeal to common sense. Frankie stared out of the windscreen as he listened to his son before interrupting him.

"I've had a fucking brainwave."

MacPherson was having a bad day, indeed a bad week and it was shaping up to be a bad month. There were dirty grey colour bags under his eyes that his latest girlfriend kept complaining about and Frankie was proving to be a distraction from all the other urgent cases he had on his desk. Last night it had been after midnight when he finished reading the latest surveillance reports and when he finally reached his bed, sleep had eluded him until the early hours. Now, he was wondering how much overtime the superintendent would allow without any results. Glancing at his watch he guessed that he would know soon enough, with a meeting scheduled for later that afternoon. Once he'd read the transcripts of the telephone calls Frankie had made from inside HMP Bleadon, MacPherson knew that things were going to get messy once he was released. Frankie wasn't the forgiving type. Frankie took revenge, quickly. It was only a matter of time.

He knew that the resources of the police service didn't

extend to continuous surveillance of a recently released prisoner. He tried re-reading the reports, but he had read them so often the words were dissolving into each other, a meaningless litany of driving and domestic arrangements. Frustration filled his mind, as he realised how little he knew of Frankie's activities since his release.

He dragged on his jacket and walked through to the conference room. He felt the crumpled remains of the cigarettes in his pocket and glancing at his watch realised he didn't have time for a smoke before the meeting.

Superintendent Baker was sitting by the table turning a silver fountain pen in his hand. He waved for MacPherson to sit down.

"Not much here."

"I know, Sir, but…"

"Don't tell me. It's a gut feeling."

"Sir. He's going to go after Locatelli."

"I'm not having police resources protecting Locatelli on the basis of your gut feeling. Locatelli's a known criminal."

"But, Sir."

After twenty minutes of persuasion that MacPherson considered to be the fundamentals of sound policing, they'd agreed on a strategy. Back in his office MacPherson actioned the plan and flicked through the latest reports about Frankie, trying to guess where and how.

The fumes from the transit filled the lock-up until Peter killed the engine and jumped out. Frankie was already standing, legs astride, by the back door of the van. He yanked open the doors and stared inside. Bungee cords, odd pieces of rope and lengths of twine hung from the wooden struts along the inside. In one corner, huddled into the foetal position, was Paolo Locatelli, his wrists tightly bound, duct tape covering his mouth.

Frankie clicked on the torch, held spear-like, in his right hand and lit up Locatelli's face – eyes wide, pupils small.

"Paolo, my old mate," Frankie said.

Peter jumped into the van and dragged Locatelli until he fell out of the rear into a heap, a faint cloud of dust rising as he hit the floor.

"Welcome to my humble abode," Frankie said.

Locatelli fumbled on the ground.

Frankie drew back his right foot and landed the first kick to Locatelli's rib cage. The pain flashed across his face, the duct tape stretched across his mouth muffling the groans of pain. Locatelli's writhing body wriggled on the floor unable to judge when the next blow would come.

And it came soon enough.

Frankie aimed the point of his brogues at Locatelli's right thigh and swung the blow. Tears drizzled down Locatelli's cheeks cascading over the duct tape and onto his chin. Peter winced as he heard the cracks of breaking ribs as Frankie landed two more blows.

Frankie dragged Locatelli across the floor before pulling him upright and pushing him onto the hard wooden chair. Frankie undid Locatelli's hands and rebound them behind the chair.

"Paolo," Frankie began. "Look what you've done to my brogues." He pointed at the scuff marks.

Frankie took a step back.

"We've got some unfinished business," Frankie said, his tone halfway between let's-be-friends and I'm-going-to-kick-the-shit-out-of-you. He turned his back and walked over to the bench, returning with a small wooden tray.

"Do you know what these are?"

Locatelli nodded.

"Of course you do," Frankie snorted. "You're Italian. That's all you eat. Fucking courgettes."

Locatelli moved his right buttock but Frankie clenched his fist and gave him a glancing blow over one eye. Frankie lowered his head until he could smell Locatelli's expensive aftershave.

"Do you know how many different sorts of courgettes there are?"

Locatelli whimpered.

"Of course you fucking do. You're Italian."

Locatelli rolled his eyes.

Frankie lent down and rummaged through the box until he found a small courgette with a large yellow flower perched on one end. With one quick movement he pulled off the duct tape. Locatelli squealed and grabbed lungfuls of air. Frankie forced his mouth open and stuffed the courgette inside, the flower dangling limply. He bent down to Locatelli's ear.

"If you bite that courgette, you're a dead man."

Locatelli swallowed hard but his eyes told Frankie he understood.

"See these," Frankie said, holding up both hands. "They've picked more courgettes then you eat in a year. For two summers I've picked courgettes and all the time I was thinking of you."

Locatelli gave out a laugh that came out like a grunt.

"Everyday my hands would be covered in this rash from the leaves that drove me mad. Off. My. Fucking. Head."

The courgette wobbled slightly.

"And then, when I'd finished my toil in the courgette house, we'd have courgettes for tea. Courgette salad, courgettes in the curry, in the stews, courgettes every fucking meal."

Frankie grabbed one of the larger courgettes from the box by his feet and began tapping Locatelli on the head.

"And I thought of you."

The flower on the courgette in Locatelli's mouth fell off and Frankie raised an eyebrow. Locatelli blinked furiously. Frankie circled him holding the large courgette in his right hand.

"Do you know where this would fit?" he turned to face Locatelli and held the courgette to his face.

"Right up your jacksie."

Frankie laughed but Locatelli didn't see the joke.

"But then I thought it would be a waste of a decent courgette."

Frankie raised it high above his shoulder and brought it down in one smooth blow onto Locatelli's head. The courgette split apart and bits careered over the dirt as Locatelli fell to the floor, dragging the chair with him. He bit into the courgette and spat out the portion in his mouth.

"Frankie. No. I can explain."

"You're not going to beg for mercy are you?"

"Frankie, please listen…"

Within seconds blood was streaming from Locatelli's nose and cuts above his eyes. When Frankie stopped, the swelling was beginning to close both of Locatelli's eyes. He stopped kicking Locatelli and pulled the chair vertical.

"Paolo, stay awake. I still need you to tell me where my money is," Frankie was breathless.

Locatelli mumbled a reply.

"Once you tell me where the money is we're going to part as friends, aren't we?"

Locatelli was panting for breath between desperate

attempts to get Frankie to stop. Blood filled his mouth, streaking his gums and his teeth. Frankie pushed him to the floor and emptying the box of courgettes began kicking them towards him.

"I hate fucking courgettes so much…"

"I can explain Frankie please."

"Time for explanations is over."

"I haven't…"

"What was that?"

"Just give me time."

"You've had three years, twenty-one days."

Frankie stepped into the shadows and picked up a baseball bat. He turned it slowly in his hand.

"Time's up Paolo," he began tapping the bat into the palm of his other hand.

He took three strides towards Locatelli, swinging the bat in his hand. As he neared Locatelli he saw a movement to his left and turned his head as the double doors crashed open and a dozen armed police officers streamed in, shouting instructions. He released the bat and it ping-ponged on the floor and rolled out of sight.

MacPherson followed the armed response team, his stab jacket a size too small forcing his shirt up around his neck. He stood as two of the officers freed Locatelli, another two cuffed Frankie.

"Frankie Long, you know the drill," MacPherson said, glancing around the lock-up. "Kept this place a secret."

Frankie straightened himself defiantly.

"I'm arresting you on suspicion of the attempted murder of Paolo Locatelli."

"They'll never prove attempted murder."

Frankie stared at the barrister willing him to disagree. The interview room had a small table with a scratched surface and four uncomfortable plastic chairs. A prison officer walked up and down outside peering occasionally through the glass partition. The barrister was clean-shaven, chin smooth, head glistening. The chalk pinstripe was sharp enough to cut cheese and he pulled on the double cuffs of his shirt until exactly the same length protruded from each of the sleeves of his suit.

"Let's look at the evidence," he said, ignoring Frankie. "We've got the statement from Mickey French who worked with you in prison. He says you were obsessed with revenge. All you ever talked about."

"He's a scum-bag."

"Then we've got Dave Hopkins, from the snooker club. Says the first thing you did on release was to plan your revenge in detail."

"No jury would believe him. He's simple."

"But what about the tapes of your conversations from prison. Didn't you realise the conversations were recorded?"

"I never said much."

The barrister raised an eyebrow. "I've counted seventy-five references to Locatelli in the last six months of your imprisonment. A few might have been understandable. But seventy-five – what do you think a jury will make of that Mr Long?"

The barrister clasped one hand over another on top of the papers on the table and dared Frankie to defy him.

"He was a business colleague…"

"That you beat to a pulp… allegedly…"

Frankie could sense he was losing the barrister's sympathy.

"And do you know how serious a conviction will be. For you and your son. Although I have to say that the prosecution will have grave difficulty succeeding against you and Peter."

"What does his brief say?"

"We've only had a preliminary discussion so far. However..."

He opened the foolscap notebook on the desk.

"The prosecutor has made a suggestion as to how we might carve up the case."

Frankie thought about carving up Locatelli and for a moment he was back in the lock up, enjoying every minute, watching the Italian toe-rag with a courgette in his mouth, begging for mercy. The barrister continued.

"It's really quite simple. They want a plea from you to the attempted murder and they'll drop similar charges against Peter."

Frankie blinked. Then he blinked again and thought about Madge. It meant he was going to die in prison. Years in a Cat A jail, transferred from one prison to another, miles from home and then a Cat B and maybe, if he was lucky a Cat C jail. He'd be an old man before he reached an open jail. He wouldn't feel her breasts touching his chest, the touch of her hand or the smell of her perfume.

But Peter would be free.

"What sort of carve up is that?"

"They've got your card marked Mr Long. That's all I can say. If you don't accept you run the risk that Peter will go down for life with you."

"He had nothing..."

"Look," the barrister cut across him. "If you take a plea you're entitled to a credit from the judge. It should bring down the minimum tariff."

"How much?"

The barrister rolled his eyes and let out a long slow breath.

"It might make the difference between a tariff of eight years and twelve years."

"So I'd be out in eight years."

"Subject to parole, of course."

"I'll be drawing my pension."

Frankie stood up, pushed the chair until it fell on the floor behind him and walked over to the glass partition. He curled his fingers into a fist and pounded the glass slowly. A prison officer stopped and gave him a quizzical look.

"We don't have much time," the barrister said.

Frankie picked at his meal with the plastic fork. The shepherd's pie was a smearing of black acrid tasting substance covered by something that passed for mashed potatoes, accompanied by boiled potatoes and bread. Back in his cell he laid on his bunk contemplating.

That bastard Mickey French had stitched him up.

And Dave Hopkins was a grass.

Fuck them all.

He heard his name shouted and dragging himself off the bunk stepped into the corridor.

"Visitor, Frankie."

Madge was sitting at the far end of the visitor's hall holding a plastic beaker of water. She stared at the tabletop turning her drink slowly through her fingers. Frankie slipped into the bench across from her and he leant over to kiss her but she turned her head to one side and his lips brushed her cheek.

"You promised me, Frankie."

"Madge. I've been stitched up…"

"I don't want to die in prison. That's what you said…"

"I know but…"

Madge got up and walked over to the exit without

looking back. Frankie took the cup and turned it in his hand. A prison officer appeared by his shoulder.

"Visit over, Frankie."

Frankie sat in the cells underneath the Crown Court looking at the graffiti on the walls. Every few minutes the toilet let out an odd gurgle. The ragged woollen blanket heaped in one corner was polka-dotted with stains and by its side were the remains of a microwaved lasagne. The flap on the cell door slid open, a face appeared, and then a loud click as the door opened. A security guard nodded at Frankie. It was a short walk to the narrow staircase leading to the dock. The barrister and solicitor sitting in front of him nodded an acknowledgement. He scanned the courtroom and caught the warm smile of achievement on the face of MacPherson. He squinted at Madge, noticing the puffiness of her eyes, the make-up failing to disguise sleepless nights. Sophie sat by her side.

An electrifying expectation pulsed through the courtroom as the judge entered.

"Stand-up," the judge said. "I have heard the eloquent plea on your behalf by learned counsel asking me to exercise as much leniency as possible. I have carefully considered all the guidelines and especially your guilty plea which, I should say, is entirely appropriate.

"However, given the aggravating features of your case, namely the cold blooded revenge-style attempt to take the life of an innocent man, I am convinced that had it not been for the work of the police you would have murdered Mr Locatelli."

Frankie's left leg began to twitch nervously; he looked over and saw the narrow smile on Locatelli's face.

"In these circumstances the only sentence I can pass is

life imprisonment. I set a tariff of a minimum of eighteen years."

Frankie heard Madge gasp.

He felt the guards grip his wrists and looking down saw the handcuffs.

"Take him down."

About the author

Stephen Puleston has been writing for many years. He has worked as a solicitor, management consultant, and now runs an online chandlery business. In 2013 he will be publishing the first in a series of Inspector Drake thrillers based in North Wales. For full details visit www.stephenpuleston.com.

The Execution

C D Mitchell

The confession hadn't made the investigation any easier.

While the deputies took Sonny Howell out to the bottoms to try to find the body, Sheriff Wilson Underwood had been under subpoena that day. He was in state court in Jonesboro to answer questions regarding the accidental death of his own daughter who died at home when his pistol accidentally discharged. He did not arrive until late in the afternoon. When he got to the Hatchie Coon Bottoms, Sonny still hadn't shown the deputies where he'd hid the body.

The investigation into the death of Wilson Underwood's daughter was officially over. The discharge of the pistol was ruled to be the fault of the manufacturer. A sealed products liability settlement was admitted into the record. Wilson had officially been cleared by the authorities, and his own healing process could now begin.

The murder of Nancy Davis, on the other hand, was not over.

The murder had shocked the community, but every murder shocked the small community of Delbert. In the twenty plus years Wilson had served as sheriff, he had investigated five murders. Four had been solved, but this was the only one that would garner a death penalty.

Nancy had dated Sonny Howell for months before she disappeared. Her parents nagged at Wilson to investigate her absence the first day she didn't come home. But Wilson knew he couldn't begin a missing person investigation just because a girl who dated the town thug didn't show up one night. A class valedictorian and homecoming queen, Nancy could have dated anyone in Jester County, and she chose the county's best chemist. Wilson knew Sonny had two different meth labs, but Sonny always seemed to be one step ahead of him.

Frank and Ellen Davis persisted, however, and on the third day of Nancy's absence, Wilson became worried.

Sonny's family had founded Delbert, Arkansas. But although Sonny may have shared the Howell gene pool, he shared none of the character that made the Howell family such prominent members of the Delbert community. Wilson knew he needed to talk to Sonny, so he sent a deputy out to pick him up.

On a three week meth binge, Sonny came to the sheriff's office and confessed immediately. His drug induced paranoia had him convinced that the law had witnessed the murder and he had no choice but to tell the truth.

Leading the deputies around in circles through the Hatchie Coon Bottoms, and laughing at them every time they thought they'd found the right spot, Sonny refused to reveal where he hid the girl. Herman Bishop, the Criminal Investigator with the sheriff's office, and Dean Witt, the Arkansas State Police investigator, had given up and called for a cadaver dog.

After arriving at the scene, Wilson talked with the officers to figure out what was going on; then he walked over to the county patrol unit.

"Come on with me, Sonny. We gonna walk out here and see what we can find," Wilson said.

"Sure, Hoss. I'll show you all over them bottoms. You just tell me where you wanna go."

"He can't find it. His brain's so fried right now he has no idea where it's at," Witt said.

"I don't believe that. These dopers can remember where they hid a quarter of meth a year ago. He knows

191

where she's at. Y'all stay up here and wait for the dog," Wilson said to Witt and Bishop. "We may be just a bit. Hey, Herman, you still got that sharp knife? Let me have it."

Herman pulled out a long-bladed folding pocket-knife and handed it to Wilson. "Watch that blade," he said. "Me and Daddy been using it to cut pigs with. I keep it with a razor-edge."

"C'mon, Sonny. Hey, Herman, grab that rubbing alcohol in your first-aid kit. Get it out for me."

Bishop chuckled and looked right at Sonny Howell before he opened the trunk of his patrol car and handed Wilson the opaque bottle of isopropyl alcohol. Wilson placed the knife and alcohol in his back pocket.

Sonny had settled down now and no longer laughed. His hands were still cuffed behind his back. Wilson grabbed him by the back of the neck and nearly lifted him off the ground. Sonny was a big, solid man, standing six feet tall in his socks. Although the meth had whittled away a lot of his girth, he still weighed over 275 pounds. But Wilson towered over his prisoner and carried him by the nap of the neck like a truant teenager. Floating on his toes, Sonny made an effort to walk along with the sheriff. They walked for about thirty minutes, deep into the woods and far back along a big, slow bend in the Big Slough.

"Your deputies lied to me. I been off the shit now long enough to realise you haven't been watching me, or you'd know where that body is. My confession was coerced."

Wilson kept dragging him along, refusing to respond. After easing into the woods they walked fast and straight for a half-mile, then Wilson cut back east and headed for the Big Slough Ditch, an old Corps of Engineers drainage dug so long ago the trees along its banks now towered nearly as high as the forest they walked through.

"I heared they let you off the hook today for killing your own daughter," Sonny said. "If I were sheriff I don't guess they'd be anyone investigating this." The prisoner snickered.

Wilson released Sonny's neck with his right hand. With an open palm that could grasp and hold a twenty pound watermelon, he brought his left hand around and slapped his prisoner, knocking Sonny flat on his back.

"Oh, you gonna have to do better than that old man," Sonny said.

Wilson smiled at his prisoner.

Sheriff Wilson Underwood walked into the witness room at the Cummins Correctional unit knowing that within thirty minutes Sonny Howell would die. Three bare block walls surrounded twenty folding metal chairs, their numbers divided in half by a narrow aisle down the middle of the room. A fourth wall of bullet-proof glass squared off the room – the black curtains hanging from the other side temporarily hid the secrets within the death chamber. Soon, the curtains would peel back from the middle of the glass so the witnesses could observe the execution. Wilson had always wondered about the bullet-proof glass. It seemed odd to protect a man condemned to die, especially during the final moments before his death. The safety glass must have been installed to protect prison employees. The black curtains made the room seem small and cramped, but any room would feel cramped that held both Frank and Ellen Davis, the parents of the victim Nancy Davis, and Beaver Howell, the father of Sonny Howell.

The testimony at Sonny's trial was conclusive. On the day she had disappeared, Nancy told Sonny he would soon be a father. She was ecstatic, but Sonny had warned her the whole time they dated: if she ever got pregnant, he'd kill her. Nancy always thought he was joking. That day he talked her into going for a drive down the levy in the Hatchie Coon Bottoms of the St. Francis River. Sonny and Nancy got out of the truck down by the Big Slough Ditch, and he hit her from behind with a slapstick – a leather pouch filled with lead shot. He'd hit her three times when he thought he might want to get laid before she died, so he stripped her clothes and raped her in the seat of his truck. Sonny wasn't sure if she had died before they had sex or during. To get the death penalty, prosecutors had to prove that Nancy was still alive during the rape. The jury believed the prosecution. Sonny had laughed and joked with the deputies during his confession – saying, "That must have been one helluva an orgasm, huh?" When he realised she had died, he began to chew on her breasts, mutilating them as he gnawed her nipples and areolas away. Covered with her blood, he dragged her out into the woods and hid her body in a brush-pile. On the way back to his truck he jumped in the Big Slough to wash up before going home to finish another batch of meth.

Inside the room, the light seemed just bright enough to see with a squint. Although the curtains behind the glass were closed, Wilson could see the bright lights on the other side. Beaver Howell sat on the right of the room up on the front row. Cora Howell, Beaver's wife and Sonny's mother, had died of breast cancer three years before Sonny started cooking meth. Beaver told Wilson at the trial he understood now why God had called her home.

Beaver sat alone.

Two rows behind him sat three men in khaki slacks

with briefcases and legal pads. Wilson assumed they were Beaver's attorneys, or reporters. He didn't recognize any of them. The trial attorneys had long since been replaced with attorneys who dedicated their lives to battling the death penalty. Wilson knew that a last ditch attempt was being made at that moment to stop the execution based upon new evidence regarding Wilson's beating of Sonny Howell.

On the first row of the left hand side sat Frank and Ellen Davis. Mr Davis wore jeans and a red flannel shirt. Mrs Davis wore black from head to toe. They sat with Mooney Marrs, the preacher from the church in Delbert, and Money's wife, Delilah. Mooney held his Bible and squirmed. Occasionally he could be heard to pray under his breath, or quietly say "Hallelujah," or "Thank-you, Jesus," like he was in church on Sunday morning waiting for the crowd to arrive.

Wilson could think of no reason to be thanking Jesus right now. He'd lost his own daughter in a freak accident when his gun went off at his home, and he knew what Frank and Ellen Davis were going through. At least they could sit on this side of the chamber and hate the man on the other side for robbing them of their daughter. When Wilson tried to look through the glass, his reflection stared back at him, reminding him that the man who took his daughter's life had never faced justice. After all the investigations had concluded, the death of Wilson's daughter was ruled an accident. That only cleared him of any criminal charges. But even worse would be sitting with Beaver Howell as the state took the life of your only son while you watched, helpless to save the boy you had raised to a man.

Both sides of the aisle hated Wilson Underwood. Wilson knew how they felt. Beaver Howell believed Wilson

195

had done his job in investigating and accumulating evidence, but the old man had sworn to take revenge on him as soon as he no longer hid behind his "Tin-badge of courage." Sonny had exaggerated the beating he'd received from Wilson. Although the jury believed the doctor's testimony that the cuts on Sonny's legs were self-inflicted, Beaver Howell believed his son.

For Frank and Ellen Davis, a guilty conviction and a death sentence weren't enough. They wanted the world to know that this man had mutilated the body of their beautiful daughter. They had also lived with the fear that at any time an appellate court could throw out the conviction because of the way Wilson had handled the investigation.

The loudspeakers in the corner of the witness chamber hovered over the room like an axe about to fall. News of a stay of execution would be announced over those speakers and would enrage one side of the room – and elate the other. But that would be none of Wilson's concern today. Outside of Jester County he had no legal authority. He wore pressed jeans and a white shirt like always, but no badge was visible. Wilson was present as an obligation to the citizens of Jester County to see this case to its final conclusion. He took a seat in the back row and tried to shrivel away into the dim light, hoping his presence would not be noticed by anyone.

At the trial, Sonny Howell claimed Wilson had beaten him and threatened to cut off his testicles for talking about the shooting death of the sheriff's daughter. Wilson truthfully denied that he threatened to cut Sonny's balls off. The sheriff testified the cuts and bruises on Sonny's back and legs were the defendant's own masterwork, a result of a psychological disorder that caused the defendant to cut

196

himself. The state psychiatrist said cutting and mutilation were common among methamphetamine addicts, and the defendant's confession that he mutilated the body of his victim proved those tendencies. The judge allowed the confession given to Bishop and Witt, but refused to allow any evidence from the autopsy of the mutilated body, including any pictures of the body or physical evidence of the rape and mutilation of the corpse, ruling that the discovery of the body was the result of abuse administered by the sheriff while alone with the prisoner in the woods. The jury still convicted Sonny Howell of rape and capital murder and recommended the death penalty. The judge followed the jury's recommendation.

Now after thirteen years of appeals and coroner's inquests, public and political scrutiny, FBI and State Police investigations, and a civil rights lawsuit subsequently dismissed when he found jailhouse religion, Sonny Howell was about to die.

The curtains opened and two prison guards rolled a gurney into the death chamber. Sonny lay strapped onto his final resting place. He raised his head and looked at the glass and squinted against the glare of the reflected light. Wilson knew he searched for his father and could tell the moment the man finally saw Beaver – Sonny's face beamed with a smile. Now standing, Beaver held his hand out to his son, the palm open, the fingers extended and spread like a five-year-old about to draw a turkey.

"I'm here son. I'm here for you. Can you see me? I'm right here." Beaver ran an unsteady hand through the thinning hair on top of his head. He leaned and reached as if to touch the glass, and a guard, standing at the front of the room admonished him and asked him to please sit down. Wilson hadn't noticed the guards and didn't know if they had come in with the gurney or been there all along. Beaver stepped back from the window, but did not sit down.

Two more white-robed technicians entered the room and began to work over the prisoner. They pulled back the sleeves on his arms and searched for a vein. With rubber gloves on their hands and emotionless precision, they worked quickly and efficiently, as if they had other places they wanted to be – like a mailman moving on to the next box. In spite of his revulsion at what he watched, Wilson found himself leaning forward, stretching his neck in an effort to see.

The technicians dabbed white cotton balls with alcohol and swabbed the spots on both arms where the IV needles were to be inserted. Wilson nearly choked as he thought of the irony, and the noise brought the attention of the room to him for just a moment.

"Excuse me," he said. As if on cue, all eyes returned to the glass at the front of the room.

After swabbing the arms, they removed the plastic from the sterile needles of the IV tubes. With military precision, they inserted a needle into each arm. Sonny's face reflected the sting, and Beaver sighed and ran his hand through his hair again. They replaced the straps around his arms; then left the room without so much as acknowledging the presence of the prisoner they had just rigged to die.

Over the speakers mounted in the corners, the warden read the death warrant. The prisoner was asked if he had any final words. A guard stepped forward and held a microphone for Sonny to speak into.

"I've had years now to think what I would say when this time came. I can't see anyone but you, Daddy. It sure is nice to see you. I'll see you again in Heaven. You'll be

198

young again next time I see ya. I been baptized, and I am right with my maker. I go to a better place. Don't cry, Daddy. They don't realise they send me to paradise. This is so much better than rotting in a cell till I die. Mr and Miss Davis, I don't see you, but I know you're there. I feel your hatred. I am sorry for what happened. Please find a way to forgive me, because without your forgiveness, I will have the blood of your souls on my hands too—"

"Excuse me, but I must interrupt this proceeding." The warden's voice echoed off the block walls. "The United States Supreme Court has issued an emergency temporary stay of execution while they examine a final appeal for the defendant."

The room that had felt so small and cramped earlier now seemed large and empty, with nothing but the void of silence filling the space. Wilson sat with his head down. He didn't understand what had happened or what was going on, but he knew he was to blame. The voice came over the speaker again.

"This is a temporary stay. The prisoner will remain hooked to the IVs. The Court will issue a decision in just a few minutes. At that point, the execution will go forward, or the prisoner will return to his cell pending further court action. Please, remain calm and in your seats. Anyone creating a disturbance or harassing anyone in the witness room will be arrested and removed from the chamber. We will notify you immediately when we receive instruction from the court."

On the left-hand side of the room the witnesses reacted with rage. Ellen Davis cried and leaned on her husband's shoulder. Wilson could hear her sobs.

"This will never end. Why can't we get justice? Let's pray. Please, let's pray."

"Hallelujah. Let's seek God's will and mercy right

199

now. Every one kneel at your chairs and go to the Lord in prayer," said Mooney Marrs. They all shifted and knelt but Frank Davis, who rose from his seat and walked to the back of the room, and Delilah, who sat stone-faced in her chair next to her kneeling husband. Frank Davis stopped in front of Wilson.

"If his execution is stayed, it will be no one's fault but yours. I don't understand how God works. It makes no sense to me. My daughter and your daughter are gone, but your worthless ass and that sorry piece of shit up there on that gurney are still here."

Wilson looked up at Mr Davis.

"I promise, Frank, I don't understand it either."

A prison guard stepped forward.

"Return to your seat, Mr Davis, and be quiet, or I will remove you from the chamber."

Frank looked at the guard and then back at Wilson. "It doesn't matter. They're not gonna execute him today." Then the man turned and walked back to his wife.

As he scanned the room, Wilson missed Beaver Howell. Then he spied the bald head of the old man. Beaver had fallen to his knees, and as tears ran down his cheeks, he prayed to the same God that the people across the aisle prayed to, asking that same God for the opposite of what they sought. Wilson sat in the back, alone, and thought of what he had done that day on the banks of the Big Slough. He should have waited for the cadaver dog. The dog would have found Nancy's body, although they would have been there late into the night. Now all of these people had fallen to their knees to pray, and the man on the gurney with the needles in his arms waited to have his life extended or exterminated by a panel of judges he had never met and would never know; a panel of judges who would rule on Wilson's actions, a man

200

they had never met and would never know. What he did wasn't right, but he'd done his job; he'd solved the crime. He'd brought the decomposing body of Nancy Davis home so the family could put it to rest and begin their grieving process. And still he ended as the scorn of everyone involved. Standing up, Wilson walked to the back of the room.

To a guard he said, "Is there a bathroom? I'm sick."

"Through that door, sir."

Wilson walked in and knelt in front of the toilet. The one-piece stainless steel seat looked clean enough to eat off. He couldn't keep the toilets at the county jail that clean. Then he emptied his stomach. After retching and convulsing, he composed himself and stood. Turning the water on at the stainless steel sink, he cupped his palm under the faucet and drank from his hand. After he rinsed his mouth and quenched his thirst, he opened the door to leave the room.

As he walked into the chamber, Wilson saw Beaver Howell walking toward him.

Beaver wasn't much older than Wilson, but today he looked old. His white hair looked like new silk at the end of an ear of corn and barely covered the crown of his head. The man was short, but stocky and powerful. Beaver had spoken in anger when he threatened Wilson, but the sheriff knew the old man as a true man of God, one who practiced what he preached and lived a good life, planting and harvesting three thousand acres of rice, corn and beans with a dozen hired hands he cared for as if they were his own.

Beaver walked up to him and stopped.

"I want to hate you so bad. I know what you did. But I also know what you could have done. Sonny told me last week that you were right. That he had forgiven you. He asked me to forgive you, too. I can't kneel and ask my saviour to spare my son's life while holding this hatred for you. So I am sorry for speaking to you in anger. And whether he lives or dies today, I will not confront you. But I will never support you for sheriff again."

"I understand they finally cleared you of blame in your daughter's shooting," Beaver said.

Wilson nodded his head in a slow, exaggerated manner and said nothing. His stomach churned, and he feared the small amount of water he'd swallowed would come up if he opened his mouth.

"That wasn't your fault. I have remembered you in my prayers."

"Thank you, Beaver. God bless you," Wilson said.

Beaver returned to his seat. Wilson thought of Beaver looking at the boy for the first time, years ago in a hospital room through a glass window in a nursery. At one moment a father marvels at the life to be lived by the child beyond the glass, at the other, a father could only think of the eternity that waits the closing of the curtain.

A squawk broke the tension in the room. The warden spoke again.

"The Supreme Court has refused to hear the appeal. The temporary stay of execution is overruled."

The warden once again read the death warrant. But Wilson did not hear the words. He watched the shoulders of Beaver Howell, shaking as he cried and prayed for his son.

Wilson knew a technician would push a plunger releasing into the IV a solution that caused the prisoner to lose consciousness. Then another drug that paralysed the lungs would be thrown into the mix. The crowd watched in silence interrupted only by the sobs of Beaver Howell and Ellen Davis.

Sonny's eyes had been closed for several minutes when his fingers twitched. Wilson thought of the hand of his daughter as he had burst into her room after his gun had exploded – her fingers extended as if she waited for someone to read her future in her palm. He remembered the severed hand of Earl Montgomery that he'd found up under the train the day Earl was run over and pulled along under the wheels of the freight cars. He looked at his own hands, big and calloused, scarred from years of abuse.

Eventually a doctor walked into the room. He listened to Sonny's heart through a stethoscope, and then peeled back each eyelid to look at the prisoner's eyes. He scribbled for a few moments on his pad, then spoke.

"The time of death of Inmate Sonny Howell is 12:51 A.M."

Then the curtains slowly closed.

The quiet of the moment felt like a heavy dew, drenching Wilson. With all emotions spent, everyone stood and stumbled toward the middle of the room to leave. Wilson heard Beaver talking to a guard about having the body picked up and brought back to Delbert for burial. That made sense. The state wouldn't want to pay for burying a prisoner. Wilson wondered if Beaver would use Mooney's church for the service. It was the only church in town, unless he went to Success, or used Lamm's Chapel, a small church with a cemetery out on the edge of the Hatchie Coon Bottoms. Somehow Wilson could not see Beaver going to the Reverend Mooney Marrs and asking him to do the service after Mooney had stood with the Davis family.

With Frank and Ellen Davis by his side, Mooney eased out the door. Delilah smiled politely at the sheriff as she walked by. Wilson walked out the door behind all

203

of the others. He lit a cigarette, nearly dropping it in his haste. His truck sat at the far end of the parking lot. The cigarette had burned down to the filter by the time he opened the door to get in, so he stood outside the door and lit another one. Prince Albert was better, but he'd bought a pack of rolled cigarettes on his way down, afraid his hands might give away his nervousness as he tried to roll a smoke.

The late November sky had cleared. Breathing produced a misty cloud of vapour. There was no moon, and he searched for the Big Dipper and Orion's Belt. He remembered watching a meteor shower recently at Delbert. As he stood and looked at the stars, he wondered what happened when we die. Do we achieve all knowledge of things of heaven and earth? What would it be like to know all of physics, to see the galaxies and stars and know their names, to understand the biochemistry that makes the human body so complex; the minerals that help us to live, and the compounds that cause us to die? He wondered if his daughter had experienced all of this when she died in his arms. He wondered what it would be like to finally close his eyes and stop breathing. Would he open them again in another world? Would she be waiting there for him, to forgive him for the accident that took her life? Did Nancy Davis wait for Sonny Howell? Or would Sonny's mother greet him?

Wilson threw the butt of his cigarette onto the pavement and got in his truck. Four hours of highway separated him from home, and he wanted to get some sleep before he patrolled that evening. Shivering against the cold, he turned up the heat. As he pulled through the gate, he saw protesters standing and holding their signs. Every time an execution occurred, they appeared from nowhere – from everywhere. Wilson was surprised there weren't more. They stood and held signs that read "Stop Allowing the State to Murder our Citizens," and "Only God can take a Life." They held candles and stood in circles with bowed heads. Wilson assumed they prayed. Everyone seemed to be praying.

About the author

CD Mitchell lives in Lafe, Arkansas, in the southern region of the United States, where he raises a flock of chickens. He has an MFA with concentrations in fiction and creative nonfiction. His work appears in many national and international literary journals, and has been nominated three times for the Pushcart Prize. He has been an attorney, a tracklayer and bridgman for the Union Pacific and Southern Pacific Railroads, competed in Memphis in May preliminary BarBQ competitions, owned his own construction company, and worked on the locks and dams of the Arkansas River from Toad Suck to Ozark. He was 45-5 with 38 knockouts as a professional boxer, and although he has been a pallbearer and a groom four different times, he has never been a best man in a wedding. CD currently teaches at Arkansas Northeastern College in Blytheville, Arkansas. He is continuing work on several collaborative projects with the Chicago photographer Jennifer Moore. CD Mitchell's website is www.cdmitchell.net and can best be accessed using Mozilla, or anything but Explorer. Email is mitchell461961@yahoo.com. He is seeking a publisher for a novel in stories and a memoir.

Index of Authors

Other Publications by Bridge House

On This Day

edited by Debz Hobbs-Wyatt and Gill James

Everyone remembers what they were doing when the shocking
news broke: when Kennedy was shot, when Princess Diana
died and when the first plane crashed into the World Trade
Centre on 9/11. Yet everyday lives continued with their own
ups and downs. This collection shows us some of those possible stories and how they are gently connected with the day's
world shattering event.

A percentage of the author royalties will be donated to International Rescue Training Centre Wales (IRTCW), who provide
search and rescue dogs to the Emergency services.

Order from www.bridgehousepublishing.co.uk

Paperback: ISBN 978-1-907335-21-1
eBook: ISBN 978-1-907335-22-8

Spooked

Why does the old lady make such a big deal about inviting young couples to dinner? Why is there a uniform up in the attic? Who is the strange girl in the film?

Then there's the printer that goes mad, the delightful house in the countryside, and the fruit machines that behave oddly at the local bingo hall.

Half the time, even though you know you're reading a collection of ghost stories, you won't know who are the real people and who are the ghosts. The characters in our stories don't either.

One thing is certain: if you dare to open the pages in this volume you'll be spooked for sure.

Order from www.bridgehousepublishing.co.uk

978-0-955791-09-3

Lightning Source UK Ltd.
Milton Keynes UK
UKOW031237030213

205753UK00008B/226/P